THE BIG WHITE HOUSE ON RUSSELL STREET

And Other Short Stories

DOYLE R. PETTY

Contents

A Note From the Author   v

Charles Briscoe   1

The Amish Attacks   9

A Domestic Disturbance   13

The Great Limestone County Heist   17

A Dog's Life   27

Out Among the Shadows   31

Fancy Funeral   41

The Big White House on Russell Street   47

About the Author   139

A Note From the Author

Most of what I write is fiction, and short stories are my favorite. There are times, however, when I feel the need to share a true story, or to reflect on a non-fictional situation. That is the case with the first three stories in this book:

The Amish Attacks is my reaction to a story I read in a publication entitled *This Day in History*. It is a true story, but one that I find ridiculously unbelievable.

Charles Briscoe In this story, I bare my soul in painfully detailing my reaction upon discovering the photo of an American hero who made the ultimate sacrifice for his country.

A Domestic Disturbance tells of a situation I witnessed from afar. I was merely an onlooker in a passing vehicle, but the situation that I witnessed continues to haunt me to this day.

To those of you who purchased this book, please accept my sincere *Thank you!*

Charles Briscoe

I SELDOM LOG onto Facebook anymore, long since sick of idiotic posts that challenge you to *share*, or to type "yes" if you really love Jesus and aren't ashamed to admit it. And for a while it was fun to touch base with people I haven't seen since high school and learn what they've been up to for the past fifty-five years and how many grandchildren they have. But the posts driven by religious foolishness and political hatred have grown tiresome. There are those, however, who post stories about interesting people and places that keep me checking in from time to time, and that's how I happened upon the photograph of Charles Briscoe.

I glanced briefly at the photo and scrolled on down the page, but something made me stop and go back. There was the smiling face of this handsome young marine who was dressed in fatigues, and the brim of his hat was turned up in front. I could see in his eyes that he wasn't posing for the camera, he was smiling at the person holding it, and it was that smile that captured my attention and drew me back for a second look. I knew right then that I would have liked Charles Briscoe, and I'd like to think he would have liked me. It is said that the eyes are windows to the soul, and if that's true, Charles Briscoe had a damn good soul.

The caption identifies him as Marine Lance Corporal Charles Briscoe, and states that he was killed in South Vietnam on January 3, 1968, in service to his country. He was nineteen years old when he died, and for the life of me, I have yet to learn how his death, or the deaths of the other 58,219 young men and women who died in that pointless war, were of benefit to this country. But this is not another diatribe on the war in Vietnam, this is about Charles Briscoe.

I took notice that he went by Charles, not Charlie or Chuck, and I suspect it was because his mother had called him Charles. And I assume he volunteered because young men were seldom, if ever, drafted into the Marine Corps. In fact, I have to assume almost everything about Charles because I didn't know him, I only wish that I had.

I Googled his name and found a blog dedicated to his memory, and that's where I learned he was from Cleveland, Ohio. Alongside the Facebook photo is one taken of him in his United States Marine Corps dress uniform and he isn't smiling; his face reflects the stern confidence that fits so well with that uniform. I *shared* the photo of the smiling Charles Briscoe to my Facebook home page so I can look at it anytime I want, and even though it always hurts a bit, I look at it almost every day.

Seeing the photo of Charles Briscoe put me in mind of Benny Underhill; US Army SP 4 Benjamin Scott Underhill of Burns, Tennessee, who was killed in Vietnam on February 15, 1968, just forty-three days after Charles Briscoe. Benny was twenty-two years old when he died. He and I weren't close, but we were on a first-name basis. We met at Austin Peay State College in Clarksville, Tennessee, when my girlfriend who was Benny's cousin introduced us. He and I routinely ran into one another at *Jumper's*, a popular watering hole in Clarksville that was jam-packed with college students on Tuesday nights because of the twenty-five-cent draft beer and free cheese.

When I think about Benny, I see the cigar stub clenched in his teeth and I remember his red 1965 GTO. Benny knew how to have a good time, and like so many of us, he let good times get in the way of his studies. His grade point average, I was told, dropped below the magic 2.0 mark, the required minimum for college deferment, and he was subsequently drafted and sent to Vietnam where he lost his life; cruel and unusual punishment for merely having a good time.

At the visitation I was introduced to Benny's parents and his older twin sisters, Lois and Lorene. I distinctly remember wanting to express my sorrow for their loss, but the words wouldn't come. Funeral home visitations often double as reunions for those who gather to pay respects, and say goodbye to a loved one whose death came as no surprise because of his or her advanced age. Small talk and polite laughter are often heard as mourners exchange memories and funny stories about the deceased, but that was not the case that day in Dickson, Tennessee. The mood was somber and the atmosphere was heavy with disbelief and sorrow over the incalculable loss.

In 1997 at the age of fifty-two, I bought a Harley-Davidson. It was my first motorcycle, and until the new wore off, I went for endless rides almost every weekend. It was on a Sunday afternoon that I was heading home on highway 70, when just east of Dickson I came upon the cemetery where Benny is buried. I parked the bike and walked row after row looking for his grave. It was one of only a few when he was laid to rest, but on that day, it looked to be hundreds. I found the bronze marker bearing Benny's name, his date of birth, February 13, 1946, and the date of his death, February 15, 1968, and it was then I realized that Benny died only two days after his twenty-second birthday. Earlier today, July 13, 2017, I visited Benny's grave again, and even though it's been almost twenty years since I was last there, my heart hurt all over again when I read the words.

To say that Charles Briscoe and I would have been friends is speculation on my part and may sound far-fetched to anyone who doesn't really know me . . . few people do. But I am a *people person* and consider myself a good judge of character. I find most people easy to like, given the opportunity, although some are far easier than others. I smile at strangers and they smile back; I don't know why I do that, I just do. That's the way I am and I'm betting that Charles Briscoe shared that same trait.

It was in February 1964, during basic training at Lackland Air Force Base, Texas, that I became friends with a kid named Thomas Roberson. It must have been our similar personalities; we laughed at the same things, we made fun of the same people and we hated every minute of our daily routine. We were the most unlikely pair imaginable; I grew up in the segregated South and Thomas was from inner-city Chicago, and he was black. We first met early one morning when we were ordered outside to police the area around our barracks, or in civilian parlance, to pick up the trash. We were given roughly ten minutes to complete the task, which was more than enough time to sneak a smoke. While walking beside one another and scanning the ground, I pulled a cigarette from my shirt pocket; I had one and Thomas didn't. I'd slipped it from the pack and planned to fire it up as soon as our Training Instructor went back inside. Thomas asked if I had another, which I didn't, so we shared. One cigarette between us was enough because we had so little time, but more importantly it opened the door to our friendship. After that, we shared a cigarette every morning and spent all our free time together. Race didn't figure into our friendship because it didn't matter to Thomas and it didn't matter to me. It came up one funny morning when I told him how surprised I was that there was no brown residue from his lips on the cigarette butt, and he complimented me on how well the collar of my fatigue shirt covered up my bright, red neck. Being friends with Thomas was easy.

It may seem odd that I'm so affected by the photo of a

young marine I never met and who was killed fifty years ago on the other side of the world. But when I see Charles Briscoe's smile, it's like he's smiling at me and I smile back. Sometimes it's through tears, but I always smile back.

The Amish Attacks

I LOVE TO WRITE. I write stories about anything I find interesting and that I think readers will enjoy. Stories sometimes come from my imagination, but most often, they come from the lives of real, everyday people. *Truth is stranger than fiction,* goes the old adage, and I find that true stories are usually funnier than anything I could ever make up.

I subscribe to, and receive a daily email from The History Channel that lists events under the heading *This Day In History*, as I'm sure many of you do. Each item is titled and underlined, and with a simple click, the story unfolds in its entirety. Sometimes I read several of the stories that garner my attention and sometimes I delete the email having read none of them. This morning, September 20,

2018, a title literally jumped off the screen, screaming for my attention.

AMISH CONVICTED IN BEARD CUTTING ATTACKS!

You didn't read that wrong, that is exactly as it appeared in the article. It goes on to say:

On this date in 2012, 16 members of a dissident Amish group in Ohio are convicted of federal hate crimes and conspiracy for forcibly cutting the beards and hair of fellow Amish with whom they had religious differences. The government classified the ruthless attacks as hate crimes because beards and long hair have important religious symbolism to the Amish who are known for their pacifism, plain style of dress and refusal to use many forms of modern technology.

The article states that several of the victims were injured because of the force used to subdue them while their beards and hair were being cut. They were also humiliated to be seen by their families and fellow Amish, shorn in such a heathen fashion.

Now I asked myself, how did this wind up in federal court? I'm sure the Amish group members on both sides took the event very seriously, but hate crimes? Really? It sounds more like an episode from an old *Ma and Pa*

Kettle movie than something that would wind up in federal court.

So, that is a good story, right? Well, here's what makes it a great story. The man who orchestrated the attack; the head of the dissident group who ordered the hair and beard cutting, his name is Mullet, Samuel Mullet. You can't make this stuff up folks. That's his name, Mullet. That puts a whole new light on the story, doesn't it.

When I read the story, I couldn't believe that someone was actually sentenced to fifteen years in federal prison for cutting another's hair and beard against his will, but when I consider that the unwanted haircut may have been a mullet, that puts a whole new light on things. If indeed, the victim was forced to suffer the indignity of having to face the world, sporting a Mullet cut, I'm not sure if fifteen years is sufficient.

I didn't make this up, I promise. Look it up for yourself.

A Domestic Disturbance

I SAW the flashing blue lights a good half mile ahead.
Envisioning a terrible automobile accident, or maybe a
standoff with someone hell-bent on suicide and
threatening to take along anyone in the way, I
instinctively slowed down and prepared to pull to the
shoulder if necessary. But when I got closer, I saw there
were no wrecked cars and no SWAT team members
brandishing automatic weapons and crouching behind
their vehicles. Parked at the curb were four police SUV's,
each with its blue lights flashing, and standing in the
driveway of the house on the corner was a police officer,
and he was talking with a woman who appeared to be in
her mid to late thirties. To merit the spectacle of all those
flashing lights, I expected to see someone lying face
down on the concrete with his hands cuffed behind him,

but that was not the case. The woman was gesturing toward a man I assumed to be her husband, who was standing in the back yard with his hands in his back pockets and his head drooped, and he appeared to be talking calmly with three police officers. *This is a domestic disturbance*, I told myself.

I continued on my way, but I found thoughts of that scene to be troubling. I wondered what could possibly have happened between those two that was so bad it required four police officers, and why were their lights still flashing? Having their home surrounded by police cars was embarrassing enough, never mind the drama of flashing blue lights that only served to draw attention to the situation. I wondered if the police had been called out of fear or out of spite, or whether the young woman had even called them at all. Perhaps it was a neighbor.

Ask any police officer and he or she will tell you that a domestic disturbance is potentially the most dangerous situation that they face. Most often it is extremely tense and can turn deadly in an instant. Tempers flare out of control when the offending spouse is enraged by the intrusion of strangers into his home. In his eyes, the police officers are sticking their noses in where they don't belong, and in an emotional state already, he turns on the police, feeling that he is defending his home and his privacy. And that, more often than not, proves to be a fatal mistake.

I was on the far side of the highway, but from what I could see, the lady standing in the driveway had shoulder-length, dark hair and she was attractive. I envisioned her fifteen pounds lighter, in a gold framed wedding photo above her mantle, or perhaps on top of the bureau in their bedroom. My imagination was taking liberties, but I'm betting my assessment was accurate. The man's back was to the highway, but I could tell his hair had begun to turn gray around the edges and I'm betting he had the beginnings of a receding hair line. I envisioned him in a black tuxedo, his hair over his ears and sporting a full mustache. They were both laughing as they fed one another wedding cake, each smearing the other's face with gobs of white frosting, and I'm betting there was also a photo of them with their arms entwined, each sipping champagne from the other's glass.

What happens to people? How does marital bliss devolve into festering hatred? What happens to cause a bed once shared by lovers to now be occupied by only one-half of the *one* that was created by the wedding vows, while the other half sleeps fitfully on the sofa. I've heard it said that familiarity breeds contempt, but I question the validity of that statement. All couples argue at one time or another, it comes with the territory. But thankfully, few require police intervention.

A week later, I was again heading east when I saw that a school bus had turned onto the side street and was stopped in front of that same house, its stop sign out and its red lights flashing. Five kids streamed off the bus, two of whom headed up the driveway past the spot where the woman and the policeman had stood talking. So there *were* kids . . . I'd been wondering. I continued on, concerned about what the evening would bring for those children.Would they witness a bitter fight or would their parents wisely spare them the pain of hearing and seeing a battle scene in their war of personal failure?

It was ironic, I thought, that neither the parents nor the children would in their wildest dreams, ever imagine that a stranger in a passing car was aware of the tension inside that house, and that he was concerned for their young family. I felt like an intruder; a voyeur of sorts, peeking into the privacy of their upturned world, and I have come to the conclusion that, in my opinion, the words, *domestic* and *disturbance* do not belong in the same sentence.

The Great Limestone County Heist

THE MULLINS TWINS, Hubert and Lester, had been in one kind of trouble or another as far back as anybody could remember. At the age of six, Lester was caught stealing empty soft drink bottles from behind Elmer Highsmith's grocery and bringing them back in through the front door and selling them to old Elmer for three cents apiece. Elmer became suspicious and started marking all the returns with a grease pen before putting them out back to be picked up by the bottling company delivery man, and that's how he caught Lester red handed.

At fifteen, Hubert had a gold mine in the platinum wire he bought from Johnny Harris. It had a loop on one end, and when he worked it down into the coin slot of a pinball machine, it racked up a credit for one game every time the loop tripped the little gizmo that nickels were meant to pass through. Between Lester and Hubert, they'd sometimes take in as much as fifteen dollars in a single afternoon and thought they were straddling high cotton until one Friday when they watched as the Wells Fargo man put a stack of twenties big enough to choke a horse into the ATM machine at Highsmith's grocery.

The machine was tucked in between the *Eat-A-Snax* display and the shelves stocked with grocery items, and it didn't take a genius to figure out that a stack of twenty-dollar bills, eight inches high, is a hell of a lot more money than you could get by stealing empty bottles or robbing pinball machines, one nickel at a time.

Over the next few days, Hubert and Lester took turns hanging out at the magazine rack, pretending they were looking at dirty pictures, while they were in fact surveilling the ATM machine to see how many people slid their credit cards into the slot and walked out with a wad of twenties. On Saturday alone, Hubert watched almost two thousand dollars go out the front door.

Lester was kicked back with his feet on the coffee table, the ten o'clock news had just gone off, and when that guy that took Letterman's place came on, he turned off the television.

"I'm sorry, I just can't watch that idiot!" he said. It was too early to go to bed and Lester wasn't sleepy anyway, so he said *yes* when Hubert asked him to ride with him down to Highsmith's to buy cigarettes.

"They close at ten o'clock," he told Hubert, but Hubert said he was out of smokes and would walk all the way to Birmingham if he had to. They'd no more than pulled out of the driveway when Hubert pulled a pack of Marlboros from his shirt pocket and fired one up.

"I thought you was out," said Lester.

Hubert didn't answer. He seemed nervous as he drove on toward Highsmith's, pumping the gas pedal like he couldn't make up his mind whether to keep going or turn around.

"Why're you drivin' like that?" Lester asked.

"Like what?" Hubert said. He sounded irritated.

"You keep pumping the gas like the truck's trying to stall or something. You run it up to fifty then you let it drop back to forty. You ain't payin' no attention to what you're doin'!"

"Just nervous I guess."

"What you got to be nervous about?" asked Lester, but

Hubert didn't answer, he just kept his eye on the road and continued pumping the gas pedal.

"I told you they was gonna be closed!" Lester said in his smug, *I told you so* way of saying things whenever he was right.

"I can *see* it's closed!" snapped Hubert. "You think I'm stupid?" He turned onto the concrete drive, made a wide circle and stopped between the gas pumps with the front end of his pickup facing the highway.

"What the hell are you doin'?" Lester screamed when Hubert put the shifter into reverse, looked into the rearview mirror and stomped the gas pedal to the floorboard. Tires were screaming and leaving black streaks on the concrete when they crashed through the front of Highsmith's grocery, completely destroying the front door, the plate glass windows on either side and the aluminum framing that held it all together. The truck came to a stop about two feet in front of the ATM machine and Hubert slipped and almost fell when he jumped out onto the floor that was slick with tomato juice, busted cans of Vienna sausages and crushed packs of peanut butter crackers.

"What the?" was all Lester managed to articulate before Hubert yelled,

"What the hell're you waitin' for? Get the damn chain out of the back and wrap it round that machine, we ain't got all night!" Lester just continued sitting in the truck, thoughtfully contemplating the situation. First of all, he didn't like being yelled at, and secondly, he thought it unfair that Hubert chose to handle things the way he did, not bothering to tell him what was about to happen. They'd talked about how much money might be in the machine, and he thought that possibly at some point they might actually . . .

"Get the damn chain!" Hubert screamed, kicking his way through cans of Rotel and boxes of Kraft Mac'n Cheese. Lester wrapped one end of the chain around the machine and Hubert hooked the other end around the two-inch ball on the trailer hitch. He threw four cartons of Salem Lights and a twelve-pack of Milwaukee's Finest onto the front seat and climbed in, dropped the shifter into low and stomped the gas pedal, gripping the steering wheel with both hands and gritting his teeth. The tires squealed and showered the place with broken glass when the truck lurched forward, uprooting the money machine, and when they cleared the building, Hubert threw the shifter into park and they both ran to the back and tried to lift the machine up into the bed of the pickup.

"This sumbitch weighs a ton!" Hubert grunted, straining

to lift the thousand-pound monster. "Get back in the truck!" he shouted to Lester, and they took off down the highway with sparks flying from the thundering steel box bouncing along the pavement at fifty miles an hour. Without slowing down, Hubert hooked a left onto the first side road he came to and almost turned the truck over when the back end slid in the gravel, slinging the heavy machine around to the right. Hubert managed to get straightened around and again pushed the pedal to the floor, leaving a cloud of dust that would have been seen for miles had it been in the daytime.

"Stop the truck!" yelled Lester, "I've got an idea. They's a steep bank on this side of the road that drops down about three foot into that field. Pull that machine over as close to the side as you can get it, then drive on down there where the bank levels out and come back through the field and back up to where the machine is. Between the two of us, we oughta be able to roll the damn thang down the bank and into the back of the truck!" Hubert was skeptical, but having no better plan, he put the shifter into park and ran to the back of the truck to help Lester untangle the chain, then he jumped back in and drove a tenth of a mile down the road and turned onto the freshly plowed ground and headed back to where Lester was waiting. Centering on the machine, Hubert watched in his rearview mirror and slowly backed up until the rear tires sank into the eight inches of mud at the bottom of the embankment. Lester used his cell phone to call their cousin Ralph, and he and Hubert were sitting on the machine, each drinking a Milwaukee's Finest and smoking a Salem Light when they heard the sound of Ralph's big John Deere chugging up the road with only one of its headlights shining.

"Damn! What'n the hell've y'all done now?" Ralph shouted. "And what'n God's name is that thang y'all are settin' on, anyway?"

"Never you mind!" Hubert yelled back. "Just drive out into that field and back up to the truck and pull me outa there, all right?" Ralph was driving the tractor through the field when the flashing blue lights and screaming sirens flew past the end of the dirt road and on down the highway and out of sight. When Hubert got the truck back up onto the road, he tied the end of the chain to the pole Ralph used to move round bales, and had him lift the machine up into the bed of the truck.

Hubert slid the door shut at the end of their grandaddy's barn while Lester turned on the lights in the hallway. They both climbed into the back of the truck, but despite all their tugging, pushing, pulling and shoving, they couldn't budge the machine. Then Lester got the bright idea to tie the chain around one of the six-by-six uprights and drive out from under the "damned thang". It hit the ground with a thud, conveniently landing with the access door facing upward.

"Now we're cookin'!" said Hubert. "Hand me that drill over there and that box of drill bits."

Hubert wore out three drill bits while penetrating less than one-eighth inch into the case-hardened steel and Lester almost gave himself a hernia straining on the crow bar that he managed to slip into the edge of the access panel. Hubert pounded on the machine with a sledge until he was out of breath and could no longer lift the nine pound hammer.

"Where's grandaddy keep the dynamite?" Lester asked.

"Oh hell no, we ain't doin' that!" said Hubert. "That's the stupidest thang I ever heard! Hell, you'd blow this place to smithereens and us with it if I wadn't here to keep an eye on you!" Then he rummaged through the room where their grandaddy kept his tools and came across an acetylene torch and a pair of dark goggles.

"Roll that tank over here!" he shouted to Lester. "And I'll show you how it's done!"

The glow from the fire lit up the night sky and could be seen all the way into town. The conflagration was classified a *two alarm*, which was the maximum on account of the town only had two fire engines, luckily both of them pumper trucks. The volunteers spent the rest of the night spraying the water they drained from the livestock pond onto the smoldering hay, cow manure and what was left of a pickup truck and something that resembled a small refrigerator.

"This was old man Mullins' barn," said Al Pritchard, the volunteer fire chief. "And that truck looks like the one that belongs to his idiot grandson, Hubert."

"Look at them dumb sumbitches!" laughed the sheriff and his deputies, watching Hubert and Lester on the video from Highsmith's security camera. "Them two couldn't pour piss out of a boot if the instructions was wrote on the heel!"

Two deputies drove out to the Mullins' place the following morning and arrested the twins, while a representative of the Diebold Company supervised a crew that hooked a chain to the ATM and dragged it out of the ashes. He slipped the key into the slot and easily opened the still-warm access door and retrieved two undamaged twenty dollar bills. Shaking his head, he mumbled something that only he could hear, and then climbed into his company car and drove away.

A Dog's Life

I WAS glad when he got rid of Rita. She used to do bad things to me when he wasn't looking, and then when he'd come back into the room, she'd pat me on the head and go on and on about what a *good boy* I was. He'd just smile and look at her like she was the grandest thing he'd ever seen, but if he'd been paying attention, he would've noticed that I never went to her when she called me. I'd go lay in a corner somewhere . . . anywhere she wasn't.

But this new girl, Joanne? She just might be worse than Rita, if that's possible. Last night I waited patiently through all the heavy breathing and shit, until he finally remembered it was way past my suppertime. He came stumbling out of the bedroom and threw a handful of the dry stuff into my bowl, then hurriedly fixed two more Margaritas and headed back toward the bedroom. He usually mixes a little ground turkey in with the dry stuff, but he has his priorities I suppose . . . so much for all that *daddy's boy* crap.

I've been with him for almost five years now and I've lived up to my end of the deal; I fetch his slippers, I run out and get his damned newspaper, rain or shine, and I keep the neighbor's tomcat chased away so it won't piss in his car like it did last year. You'd think he'd learn to keep his windows rolled up!

I'll never forget the day he and this girl . . . I can't remember her name, but she was the one before Rita, or maybe the one before that. Anyway, they came into the shelter and *she* picked me out. He wanted this cute little terrier-mix, but nothing would do her but to get me. And that would've been fine with me except these other people who had this really cute little girl had already picked me out, but they had to go back home first because her daddy had forgotten his credit card. Well, I couldn't tell 'em that these other people were coming back to get me, and nothing would do . . . damn, why can't I remember her name? Anyway, her mind was made up so I had no choice but to go with them. Don't get me wrong, for the most part everything's been ok, but I think about that little girl a lot.

You know what else? He fell for that television ad where

this folksinger, Sarah somethingorother, is singing this
song having to do with an angel's arms, or something like
that, and they show this brown and white dog that's in a
cage. There's snow and shit everywhere and he's
shivering. She's singing and there's this phone number on
the screen you can call to sign up to send in nineteen
dollars a month to help get this dog in out of the snow
and get him some food. You know the ad I'm talking
about? Anyway, did you get a good look at that dog? He's
fat! I mean this sonofabitch is fat and slick and there ain't
no way he's been living in that cage out'n the snow with
nothing to eat. My guess is that he belongs to the guy
who shot the video. He probably snatched him up out of
his 5th Avenue flat and put him in that cage just long
enough for him to get good'n cold so he'd start shivering!
Then soon's he got all the footage he needed, he wrapped
him up in a blanket, or whatever, and put him back in his
Land Rover, and away they zipped back to his cushy
apartment! Anyway, think of the chew toys and stuff he
could buy with the nineteen bucks he sends them people
every month.

I love it when it's just me and him cause I get to go with
him in the car and we eat at that place where this girl on
roller skates brings out the food. He pinches off pieces of
his hot dog and shares 'em with me. But now he's wooing
this new bimbo, so I have to stay behind because the

drive-in place ain't good enough for her. He could feed her hot dogs and fries like he eats when it's just me and him, but noooo, she's got to go to this fru fru place and eat lettuce cause she's one of *those.* Did you ever see anybody bring home a doggie bag full of leftover lettuce?

Well, they don't know it yet, but I won't likely have to put up with this one after tonight. I sneaked into the bedroom while they was doin' it, and I pooped right beside the bed where when she gets up she's gonna step in it. Being liquored up'n all, she won't look first, she'll just put her big number ten right in the middle of it and then it'll hit the fan. She'll scream and holler about *that friggin dog,* and about how this place is a pigsty! He'll whine about how he *just can't seem do anything to please her*, then she'll make him take her home, which he'll do, and then he'll come back and start in on the tequila. And that's good, cause when he gets to drinkin' all by hisself, he gets all chummy with me. He'll pat the sofa cushion and say, *c'mere boy*, and I get to lay down and put my head in his lap. He'll feed me Fritos and stuff, and that's when I know for sure he loves me. At least until somebody new comes along and shakes 'em in his face, and then here we'll go again! But til that happens, I'm gonna lay right here on the couch and enjoy myself.

Out Among the Shadows

NIGHT COMES FAST in late October. Moonlight and howling coyotes bring to mind scenes from old John Ford westerns, and the magic of Bernstein, heralding the majesty of the West.

Jake Littleton was kicked back on the front porch, his heels on the railing, enjoying the coyote serenade and the stillness of the evening when he heard something rustling in the brush just beyond his field of vision. The dogs were restless and began pacing back and forth. The hair was standing on their backs, but not one of them ventured down the steps and out into the darkness to investigate. Old Dan, the biggest and boldest of them all was standing by the front door, panting and staring at Jake. He was worried . . . he wanted to go inside. That unnerved Jake because of all his dogs, Dan was the boldest and the most intelligent.

Jake couldn't pinpoint exactly what time he fell asleep, but it was well after midnight. He went to bed a little before ten, but tossed and turned with every tick of the wall clock in the living room, and he remembered hearing twelve chimes. The sun glowed red on the insides of his eyelids as it streamed through the window. The dogs were all asleep on the bedroom floor except for Dan, who was lying on the bed at his and Laura's feet. Dan knew he wasn't supposed to be on the bed, but he was sleeping soundly, apparently unconcerned with the house rules. The old rooster routinely took his place atop the corner fence post to announce each new day, but if he had crowed this morning, Jake had slept through it. In fact, he hadn't crowed the morning before, nor had he been seen all day, but neither Jake nor Laura had noticed.

He got up to put on the coffee and almost tripped over Dan who'd followed him into the kitchen without his noticing. When he filled the pot with water and turned toward the coffee maker, there was Dan, panting and looking worried. That wasn't like Dan . . . nothing ever rattled him, at least not until the night before.

Jake poured his first cup, then took down his daddy's old Winchester and leaned it against the wall by the door as he headed out onto the porch. There's nothing like the first cup, fresh mountain air and the view from the porch. The hens were scratching about, busily pecking little treats from the grass, but he didn't see the old rooster. Within minutes Dan was sleeping soundly at his feet even though he'd just awakened from an eight-hour slumber.

Jake finished his second cup, then headed to the henhouse to gather eggs, and just before he reached the door to the coop, something caught his eye in the tall grass around to the side. He headed that way for a closer look, then a chill went over him before he knew for sure what it was he was seeing, but he instinctively knew it wasn't good. He stood over the clump of reddish-brown feathers and stared at the splattering of dried blood on the weeds; it was old *Foghorn Leghorn,* his pet name for the rooster. His heart sank. Foghorn was just an old rooster, but he'd become a fixture around the place.

Dan busily sniffed the ground, then looked toward the tree line and whined like he had the night before. Usually he'd go tearing out toward the trees in a dead run in pursuit of a varmint, whether real or imagined, but not this time.

Jake went back into the cabin to find Laura at the kitchen table, staring into her favorite mug.

"Want some breakfast?" he asked as he set the basket of eggs on the counter.

"Not just yet," she answered, "not until I finish my coffee." "Why is the rifle by the door?" she asked. "Are you going hunting?" She said that jokingly because Jake didn't hunt. His daddy's old Winchester had brought down many a deer in its day, but neither of them cared for venison. And besides, Jake couldn't bring himself to kill anything, he didn't have the heart. He hadn't mentioned the noise in the brush the night before, nor the old rooster because he didn't want to alarm her . . . not just yet.

"No particular reason," he replied. "I just gave it a good cleaning and oiling and checked to make sure it's loaded, just in case." Laura made no more mention of the rifle. Unlike some women, she was comfortable around guns. She was proficient with the Winchester and had spent countless hours target shooting. She was capable of obliterating the bull's eye on a paper target and would flash a confident smile afterward. But it was only paper; Laura couldn't bring herself to kill anything either.

Jake was mending fence several hundred feet down the hill behind the tool shed that blocked his view of the cabin. He heard Big Blue, his Tennessee Blue-Tick hound, barking and raising hell like he'd treed a whole family of raccoons. Jake paused for a minute, then shook his head and laughed. Dan was right there beside him and he had no idea where the other two dogs were. Blue was the only one making a ruckus and it didn't surprise Jake in the least, Blue was young, aggressive and had one hell of an imagination. Sometimes in his sleep, his legs would jerk back and forth in a running motion and he'd make these funny noises that sounded like a mixture of barking and whining as he chased some critter in his dreams. Dan wasn't so easily excited. He was older and more experienced, and when he slept, he slept soundly. The only sound that ever came from Dan was his snoring.

Jake put his fencing tools away and headed for the house. Dan had run ahead and was waiting on the porch, standing next to Blossom, the stray who'd wandered in half-starved three weeks earlier. Blue was down by the edge of the woods, but he wasn't barking. The hair was up on his back and he was staring into the thick brush. He was standing stone still. Billy, the Redbone-Bloodhound mix, was nowhere to be seen.

"C'mon Blue!" shouted Jake, but the dog ignored him. "Ok, big boy," he muttered as he closed the door behind him. "I bet you'll come in when you get good and hungry."

Jake was awakened by a thud of some sort, or maybe it was a whack. At least he thought he'd heard something and was lying quietly, waiting to hear it again. Then he began to doubt if he'd heard anything at all; perhaps he'd been dreaming. The wall clock chimed three times as he rolled out of bed and tiptoed to the window, pulled back the curtain and peered out into the darkness. For an instant he thought he saw movement out there among the shadows, but he couldn't be sure; perhaps it was the wind stirring the leaves. He went to the front room and peered through the panes on the upper half of the door and could definitely see movement out on the porch. He flipped on the light and there was Blue, his front legs dancing in anticipation of coming inside. He bolted through the doorway and stood close to Jake. He was shivering, even though it was a warm night. Then he ran to Jake and Laura's bedroom instead of to his food bowl, which was puzzling because he had to have been starving. But evidently, he was more scared than hungry.

Several days and nights passed uneventfully. The moon was full and it was said that predators won't move about freely in the moonlight. Jake questioned the validity of that statement, but then he didn't know for sure. It made sense that a skulking animal wouldn't stray out into the moonlight where it could easily be seen, but how would an animal know that? Especially if it were at the top of the food chain and had no fear of anything . . . except man, of course.

Jake drove into town to pick up a few things at Jensen's, then headed over to the feed store for fifty pounds of cracked corn for the chickens. George Webber was holding court over by the Coke machine, telling the regulars about finding one of his calves that had been slaughtered and dragged into the woods.

"He was ripped to shreds and half-eaten when I found him," said George. "The blood was still fresh and he was warm, so whatever done it couldn't have been too far away. The Wildlife Resources officer told me it looked like the work of a big cat, but he said there'd been no big cats around here for nigh on eighty years, at least none that anybody's seen. Whatever it was had to have been big," said George. "That calf weighed almost five-hundred pounds!"

Jake didn't tell 'em about ole Foghorn; a dead rooster wasn't big news compared to George's half-eaten calf. He loaded the bag of corn into the bed of the truck and headed on back home. The sun was straight overhead now and it was starting to get hot, at least for October. That's what he loved about the fall, cold nights and warm days. *That's what makes the leaves bright*, he said to himself. *Cold nights and warm days.*

He pulled to the left side of the road and opened the door to the mailbox. It was early, but he always stopped to check, sometimes the mail came early. He pulled into the yard expecting to see the dogs running to greet him, but none came.

Must be running a deer or a coon, he figured, then he saw Blue lying on the ground, not fifteen feet from the front steps. He bolted from the truck and ran to the dog who was badly hurt and covered in blood. His eyes were open but they weren't focused and he was barely breathing. He saw the spent 30-30 cartridge on the ground, then took notice that the front door was standing wide open. He yelled for Laura, but got no answer. He ran up the steps and into the house, searching room to room, but Laura was gone . . . and so was the Winchester.

He went to the chest of drawers and pulled his Smith and Wesson .357 magnum from beneath the underwear, then gave the cylinder a spin to be sure it was loaded. He was sweating profusely and his hands were shaking almost uncontrollably as he headed down the steps.

"Come on Dan, let's go!" he said, but when he reached the tree line, he turned to find that Dan wasn't with him.

He looked back toward the cabin and saw the old dog standing on the porch and staring at him.

"Come on Dan!" he shouted, slapping his hand against his pant leg, but Dan didn't budge. He just stood there on the porch and watched as Jake headed into the forest alone.

Fancy Funeral

I HAD to hold the knob steady with one hand and jiggle the key just right to get the front door to open. Most of the time it's easy, but today it was more trouble than usual. Maybe it was just me, I don't know. We'd just buried mama and I wasn't in no mood to hassle with the doorknob, or anything else for that matter. I'd been after mama forever to get Joe Dugger from down at the hardware to replace the lock, but that was so far down her list of priorities, it didn't stand a chance. When I finally swung the door open, a gust of wind sent dust particles dancing into the sunlight streamin' in over the dining room table. That was my fault. I'd volunteered to vacuum mama's trailer for her, but it had been weeks since the last time I'd done it. In my defense, though, I'd put it off because the place was cluttered and hard to clean. The table was full size and not intended for a mobile home, it just barely fit into the space between the kitchen and the living room and you had to turn sideways and squeeze between it and the wall just to get by. But nothing would do mama but to have that table.

She made a deal with Earl Mackey down at the furniture store to let her pay for it over time, and even though it took her almost three years, she paid him every last cent. Of course Earl made it easy on her as he could, he didn't charge her no interest and he didn't get all worked up if she made a payment late. That's how mama was, she didn't have a lot but what she had was the best she could afford. I guess that's why she spent every last penny of her savings on her funeral, she wanted to go out in style just like Myra Townsend.

Mama had never talked about her own funeral until she went to Myra's back in 2012. When daddy died in 1994, she had him buried in the economy plywood model like the county buries the homeless in over at the potter's field by the sewage treatment plant. It wasn't that she didn't love daddy, it was just that back then she didn't give much thought to how you leave this world and she couldn't see no sense in buying an expensive coffin just to bury in the ground and never see it again.

Of course that was before she saw Myra laid out in that

oak coffin. Somehow, all the ceremonial pomp gave Myra
an air of sophistication she never had in life. That oak
casket was the first one any of us ever seen that was made
out of real wood, other than that plywood coffin daddy
was buried in of course. And the pall of white roses,
Lordy there must have been fifty of 'em. It was a sight,
the likes of which you never seen, so then of course,
mama had to have seventy-five red ones in hers.

Why Myra Townsend? Myra and mama were never what
you'd call friends. They weren't close at all, and if the
truth be told, mama probably didn't even like Myra. I
think it was because Myra had things and mama didn't.
They hired in at the same time down at the cotton mill,
but Myra married better'n mama, leastways when it came
to money. Joe Townsend took a chance and borrowed
money to open a grocery store down on Centennial
Boulevard, and he struck gold when he started making
sandwiches back at the meat counter. The store filled up
at lunchtime every day with workers from the cotton mill
and the hardwood flooring plant just up the street. They
stood in a line all the way from the front door to get
boloney, or ham and cheese sandwiches, potato chips and
soft drinks. Before they knew it, Joe and Myra had a
bundle of money in the bank and bought a house in
Sylvan Park, over on the other side of Charlotte Pike.

Mama had a hard life. She grew up poor in a sharecropper family and knew nothing but hard work and hand-me-down clothes. Then, when she married daddy and moved to town, she felt like she'd been delivered from the gates of Hell because she didn't have to work in the blistering hot fields any more. Of course she didn't know it was hotter'n blazes inside the mill in the summertime and colder'n a mother-in-law's kiss in the winter. But she was happy. Daddy was good to her, and she told me once that when she had me, her life was complete . . . she had everything she ever wanted.

She didn't look like herself in pink chiffon with her hair all done up. She never wore it like that when she was alive, but she looked more like Myra had looked in her oak casket, except better, because mama's was mahogany. I guess she never got that image of Myra out of her head because it seemed like she was trying to outdo her, or at least match her final splendor. That, and the way the crowd went on about how good Myra looked must have made an impression on her that she never forgot.

I don't know what made mama think she had to have such a fancy funeral for people to remember her in a good light; she was never uppity in life and didn't seem to place any importance on making a big impression on anybody. But somehow she got it in her head that people's memories of her would be better if she was wearing pink chiffon rather than a plain cotton house dress. She'd have died a second death if she'd known there was only fourteen people at her funeral, and that only eight of them went on to the cemetery. And she didn't know I borrowed almost four thousand dollars to pay off the funeral home and that it'll take me a couple of years to pay it back. But that's ok . . . it was for mama.

The Big White House on Russell Street

GOD CLOSED His eyes and gave the world a spin. He
balanced it on the tip of his index finger like a Harlem
Globetrotter, and when it stopped, He blindly jammed His
finger into the red dirt and declared it the shittiest place
on earth! Leastways, that's what her granddaddy told her
when she was little . . . it was his way of explaining the
giant sinkhole at the back of the property. "Lincoln
County is pretty as any place on earth," he used to say,
"unless you're a sharecropper."

Della Borden was born just north of the Tennessee-
Alabama line, the ninth of ten children. She was the third
of four girls, had five older brothers and a stillborn who
was buried unnamed. She didn't learn about the one
who'd died until she was in her teens, and she wasn't told
its gender, but she considered it the lucky one. They all

lived in a tiny house set smack in the middle of an open field over one-hundred yards from the nearest shade tree, and with the exception of the sinkhole, every square inch was covered in cotton.

Her daddy died when she was three years old and she had no memory of him other than the photograph her mother kept in the cedar chest. He was tall and thin, had a mustache, deep-set dark eyes and was easy to look at. She knew nothing about him other than he'd fathered ten children, and she couldn't help but wonder if they'd been conceived in love, or to merely increase the work force. There had to have been a mutual attraction at some point, but it was hard for Della to visualize him and her mother that way; he looked to be twenty or so when that picture was taken, and her mother, now fifty, was stoop-shouldered, wrinkled, and her teeth were all gone. There was no photo to prove she was once young and pretty, and Della's imagination just wasn't that good.

When her daddy died, her mother had to step up and take his place in the fields in order to hang on to the house. They'd have a place to live so long as the crop was brought in on time, and then sometime in early November, the landlord would come around with her share of the money . . . that's why they were called sharecroppers. The system worked like a fine watch, kept wound by the impoverished workers who had no place else to go. But fail to bring in a crop on time, they'll set your belongings out by the highway and move somebody in who will. And for a widow left with only four girls, bringing in a crop was damned near impossible.

When the war broke out, the boys were all called up one by one: Franklin, Lawrence, Jesse and Henry all went into the Army and Martin volunteered for the Navy to keep from being drafted. He figured sailing the high seas would be easier than traipsing all over Europe in the snow, but they didn't own a radio and he'd never heard of Pearl Harbor.

Della liked school, she'd have been a fool not to. Lincoln County schools didn't start until October because all the kids were needed in the fields. She and her little sister, Francine, attended Cash Point Elementary until mid-April when they were let out to help with the planting. Then they'd spend the next five months in the blistering heat keeping weeds chopped from between the plants. None of her siblings had gone past the seventh grade because there was no money for textbooks, but by then they could all read and write and knew a little arithmetic, so it was enough . . . it was all they needed.

The walk to school was just short of three miles but was a picnic compared to a day in the field. The schoolhouse was always warm in the wintertime because, unlike at home, there was lots of firewood. Her brothers were plenty big enough to keep the wood box filled, it's just that there were no trees on the place they were allowed to cut, and they barely kept from freezing at night with the meager supply the landlord provided.

With the boys gone, Maureen, Nora, Della and Francine were the only ones left to help in the cotton, but Maureen, the oldest, was weak and often disoriented because of a childhood bout of pellagra. Thankfully it was diagnosed early by a school nurse who explained to Inez, Maureen's mother, that the disease was caused by a nutritional deficiency brought on by a steady diet of dried beans and corn meal.

"Don't you raise vegetables in your garden?" asked the busybody woman. Inez answered her with a simple, "Ain't got no garden."

Maureen was the way she was on account of the disease, but Nora had been slow since birth. They sent her home just a few weeks into the first grade saying there was just no point. She was abnormally heavy for a girl her age and was more of a hindrance in the field than help, but she liked to cook, and by the age of twelve she was doing most of the cooking and household chores. That left only

Della and Francine to help in the cotton . . . and that's how they wound up in Nashville.

The landowner had a brother who owned a few rental houses in the West Nashville neighborhood known as *The Nations,* and he arranged for Inez and the girls to move into one that was currently empty. The long, narrow *shotgun* house was one of three that set side by side facing Centennial Boulevard down where the streetcar tracks ended near the penitentiary. The area was called The Nations because all the streets running east and west were named for states of the Union, and because the area was part of the Chickasaw Nation when white men first arrived. Inhabited by mostly poor, white, working-class people, The Nations was a great place for kids. Hordes of them roamed the streets at will with no one fretting over where they were or what they were doing because they always showed up at suppertime tired, dirty and hungry.

Inez received an allotment check each month from her boys in the military that was almost enough to pay the rent. Maureen found work at a shirt factory close in to town, and Della, who wasn't quite seventeen, went to work at the cotton mill down on 63rd. Between the two of them they brought in enough money for food and incidentals. Francine was still in school and Nora did the cooking and saw after Inez who at sixty, was for all practical purposes an invalid.

Della reported for work thirty minutes early on her first day at the mill where the shift foreman teamed her up with Beatrice Fuller, a twenty-five-year-old divorcee who'd worked in the mill going on ten years. Beatrice could do the job as well as any man there, and better than most. She was outspoken and shared her opinions freely, whether solicited or not. She was a realist and met life head-on as her needs dictated and her conscience allowed. She always sought to do the right thing, but not necessarily at the right time; sometimes she simply didn't have the will power. She was a looker, what with her red hair, her bright blue eyes and the body of an eighteen-year-old, but it was her face that captured men's attention. She looked like the angel that she wasn't and was pursued constantly by a legion of would-be lovers. She was street-smart, though, and not easily taken in . . . she'd heard every line of bullshit imaginable.

Della took her place on the production line, intimidated by the unending rows of the thingamajigs that spun cotton into thread and then wound it onto large wooden spools. It was unbearably hot inside the mill and the air was thick with lint that hung over the workers like a fog.

"Here, wrap this around your face," said Beatrice. "You don't wanna breathe in that stuff, you'll get brown-lung."

"Brown lung?" Della asked. "What's brown-lung?"

"That's when lint clogs up in your lungs til you got no room left for air and it smothers you. I've seen people in their last days, and I'll tell you honey, it ain't a pretty thing to watch." She handed Della a strip of a cheesecloth-like material like the one swirled around her own face and head, leaving only her eyes showing and looking like a character from an old Valentino movie.

Della had worked in cotton since she was big enough to walk. By age six, her feet were toughened by the sunbaked red dirt, her back and arms were burned brown and her fingers were scarred from the bracts that were like tiny spear points, put there by God to protect the delicate white fiber. She once thought nothing could be worse than working in a cotton field, but now it was a toss-up; inside the mill she was out of the sun, but it was hotter than a foundry and the clatter of machinery was deafening. She arrived home after her first day, stinking of sweat and her hair gray with the lint that made her look like the old woman she felt like, and she was too tired to eat. The following morning, Della took her place at the production line, her face and head wrapped tightly in the arabesque garb. She bid a good morning to Beatrice, who barely had time to reply before the machinery started up, making conversation impossible.

Della was sitting alone at the top of the rear steps of the building, eating her lunch of Vienna sausages and soda crackers, when Beatrice plopped down beside her and fired up a Camel.

"Hey there little sis!" she said. "Haven't had much of a chance to chat with you, what with the noise and all. Tell me your name again, I'm not sure I heard it right."

"Della," she said, extending her hand. "And I never thanked you for the facecloth, so thank you . . . you saved my life yesterday. They didn't tell me I needed one when I hired on."

"There's lots of things they didn't tell you honey. These people don't give a shit about you or anybody else. To them you're a name on an index card, and as long as you keep those spools changed out, they'll keep writing you a check every Friday. And it don't matter to them who it's made out to, just so the work gets done. Remember that and you'll be fine. Here, you want a smoke?" she asked, flipping the pack forward.

I don't smoke, Della almost said, but she stared at the pack trying to decide . . . she'd always wanted to try it.

"Oh, why not?" She shrugged and reached for the one that had popped up with the flick of Beatrice's wrist. One drag later, Beatrice was rocking back and forth, slapping her knees with both hands and laughing at Della's convulsive coughing and gagging. She apologized when the fit was over and Della regained her breath.

"I'm sorry honey, why didn't you just tell me you don't smoke? I had no idea."

"It's kinda like eatin' sardines," said Della."Everybody makes it look so good, I just wanted to try it. How do you stand it?"

"I guess I've been doing it for so long now, I forgot what the first one's like."

Beatrice and Della began meeting on the back steps for lunch every day and soon became friends. Della, in her *down-home* naiveté hadn't noticed, but she was getting looks from practically every man at the mill.

"They sure are checking you out, honey," said Bea.

"Who's checking me out? What are you talking about?"

"The men, Della-Doo, who do ya think?"

"Which ones?"

"All of 'em for Christ's sake! Where're you from anyway, Podunk?"

"Where's that?" Della asked with a straight face. "I never heard of Podunk, I'm from down around Ardmore."

"Same thing," Beatrice said. Then she let out a belly laugh and put her arm around Della's shoulder.

And the men were *indeed* checking her out. Most of them were married, but that didn't seem to matter. Whenever Della saw one of them ogling her, she'd look at his left hand to see if he was married, but since wearing jewelry in the mill was prohibited for safety reasons, it was nearly impossible to tell who was and who wasn't, except for the ones who had the telltale white circle around their otherwise tanned ring finger. But when Ernie Preston started looking her way, suddenly it didn't matter. As it turned out, Ernie was single and he made a point of getting Della's attention every morning with his big, toothy grin. Ernie was handsome and he knew it.

"So what's up with you and Ernie?" Beatrice asked, one day during their lunch break.

"Nothing," Della answered, "at least not yet. But every time I look up, he's staring at me. It's kinda weird," she confided in Beatrice, "he always has this *look* on his face . . . like I was naked or something. But, so far, he ain't said a word to me, he just stands there and grins. Reckon he can talk?"

"Oh he can talk all right, he's just bidin' his time. He's workin' his charm on you, and when he thinks the time's right, you'll see how much he can talk and just how good he is at it!"

"Sounds like you're talking from experience." Della said. Beatrice just stared at her feet.

"Yeah," she said, finally. "We had a little fling a couple a'years back, nothing serious. Oh he started out hot'n heavy like he's doin' with you now, and he couldn't have been any nicer. He even invited my kid to come along a few times on Saturday afternoons. He'd fill him up on Krystals and ice cream, then take us over to Centennial Park and turn him loose on the playground. He was a regular *mister homebody* til he got what he wanted, and then when he'd had all of it he wanted, he dropped me like I had dog breath or something." She then turned her head and wiped the moisture from her eyes that she didn't want Della to see. "And you know, I handled it just fine, I'm a big girl, but my son, Denny, he really liked Ernie and was beginnin' to look forward to seein' him . . . then he just quit coming around. It really hurt Denny's feelings . . . it was kinda like he thought it was his fault."

"When he got what he wanted? You mean you let him . . . you slept with him?"

"That's right honey, you guessed it. Wow, you are quick! You caught on to that real fast!"

"You're making fun of me, aren't you."

"Why no honey, of course not . . . well, maybe just a little, but I didn't mean nothin' by it."

"But why did you? . . . oh, I'm sorry that's none of my business. I don't mean to be nosy."

"It's ok honey, it's not like I'm *Saint Beatrice* or something. And besides, he didn't do anything I didn't want him to; I got needs too, you know. I just don't know why he never asked me out again, it wasn't like I was trying to trick him into marrying me or anything."

"Well that does it!" said Della. "If he *does* ask me out, I'm not going!"

"Whoa cowgirl, hold your horses! Don't turn him down on my account, I got no hold on him, and it ain't like I'm grievin' over him either. If he asks you out, go, you'll have a good time. Just don't let him get you liquored up."

"Don't worry bout that!" said Della. "I don't drink."

"Yeah? Well, you didn't smoke either til I offered you that cigarette!"

It was just before four a.m. on the Sunday morning following Della's fourth date with Ernie and she was lying in bed, wide awake, mourning her lost virginity.

It was that second drink, the nagging voice in her head kept telling her. *You should've listened to Bea.*

At lunch on Monday, Beatrice could see that something was bothering Della. She'd hardly spoken all morning and she'd barely made eye contact.

"How was your weekend?" Beatrice asked, knowing the answer already, judging by Della's *whipped dog* demeanor.

"I should've listened to you," she said. "One minute I was sitting there sipping on the Jack and Coke Ernie fixed for me and the next thing I know, he was all over me."

Della continued to see Ernie, each date ending like the one before, lying in his bed listening to him snore and feeling dirty and used, not to mention unsatisfied.

"That's just the way they are," Beatrice told her, "every damned one of 'em! They come on strong, always in such a big hurry and they don't let up til you give in. Then it's wham bam thank you ma'am and they roll over and go to sleep. I don't guess it ever crosses their midget minds that maybe you'd like a happy ending too. It's all about them! But they're all just alike, honey so I guess one's as good as another in that department. Just be happy if you settle down with a man who'll work and can hold down a job."

Della's conscience was eased somewhat when Ernie told her he loved her and started dropping hints about marriage. As they grew closer, she began to trust him and believed she was talking to sympathetic ears when she confided in him that she had been molested by two of her brothers when she was thirteen.

"They said it was my fault for paradin' around in front of 'em half naked," she told him, "but I never did that, I swear." Ernie drew her close and held her tightly as she wept.He told her how sorry he was for the indignity she'd suffered, especially that it was at the hands of her own brothers. He promised to always be there for her and to love and protect her. Della was hopelessly in love with Ernie and believed everything he said, especially the *always* part.

"You did what?" Beatrice exclaimed. "For God's sake, Della, why in the hell would you ever tell Ernie something like that?"

"Because I trust him, Bea, he loves me." Beatrice rolled her eyes and reached for a cigarette.

"Tell me again honey, where is it you're from? I hate to be the one to break it to you, but men don't love nobody but theirselves; they only need women for sex and to cook and clean for 'em. God, you shouldn't have told him that, honey, men can't handle that kind of stuff. It's ok for them to hop from one bed to the next, but when it comes to settlin' down with a woman, she damn well better be a virgin! That's how they are . . . how many times have I told you that!"

"Ernie's not like that, he knows what happened to me wasn't my fault, he'd never hold something like that against me."

"So what's up with you and Ernie?" Beatrice asked, chewing on her tunafish sandwich in between puffs on her cigarette. Della lowered her head and started to cry. "It's that new girl, ain't it?" said Beatrice. "I seen him gawkin' at her last week, and it ain't hard to tell what's going on. Believe me, I've been there."

"I didn't hear from him all last weekend and he's been ignoring me at work. And when I asked him this morning if there was something wrong, he just said it would be better if we didn't see one another anymore. Well, when he said that, I about lost it. I asked him why, but he just hemmed and hawed until I pushed him harder. Then he finally told me it's because I'm damaged goods . . . that's what he called me, Bea, *damaged goods!* He said he couldn't help feelin' that way, it's just the way he was brought up. Then he had the nerve to tell me he really loves me but he just can't settle down with a woman who's been with somebody else. I wanted to kill him! Then it wasn't fifteen minutes til I seen him flirtin' with that new girl just like he used to do with me."

Della lowered her face onto her upturned palms and sobbed like her heart was broken, which indeed it was. Beatrice lit a second cigarette from the butt of the first and rubbed Della's back to console her like she would a child.

"You go ahead honey," she said. "Get it all out. You grieve over that son of a bitch all you need to, but once you get him outa your system, I don't wanna see you crying over him, or any other man ever again. I'm tellin' you kid, there ain't a single one of 'em worth having! You listen to what I'm telling you!"

A week or so later, Della went out with another *would-be* suitor named Billy Caudill. Billy worked at the mill and had shown an interest in her shortly after she came to work, but he backed off when he found out she was dating Ernie. Then, when he found out that she and Ernie were no longer an item, he popped up and asked her out. Without even buying her dinner, Billy headed straight to Percy Warner Park, a secluded nature-trail on the western side of town where he parked beside a picnic area and proceeded to paw at her.

"Stop it!" she screamed, and finally had to threaten him with a nail file to hold him off.

"You didn't act so high and mighty with Ernie!" he yelled at her, "Yeah, I know all about you and Ernie!" then he called her a filthy name, started the car and drove her home without another word.

"What makes 'em like that?" Della sobbed. "Why do they think they can do anything they want . . . like you're a piece of meat?" Beatrice just shrugged.

"Your guess is good as mine, honey, but if you figure it out, I'd appreciate it if you'd let me in on it."

Days passed in silence during lunch on the back steps until finally an exasperated Beatrice turned toward Della.

"Honey, you gotta snap out of it . . . think about it this way; Ernie's a dog-ass and so is Billy, and it's best you found it out now. What if you'd married one of 'em? They're both just like my ex, neither one of em's capable of being faithful to one woman. Donnie Ray cheated on me from day one, though I didn't find out about it for a long time. He tied me down with a kid, and don't get me wrong honey, I love Denny more'n anything in the world, but Donnie Ray tied me down, then he run off with this little slut he met down at Redmond's. But you know what? She done the same thing to him, and the happiest day of my life was when he come crawling back, beggin' me to let him come home, cryin' about how much he missed Denny and me."

"So what'd you do?"

"Are you kiddin' me? I told him to go *you-know-what* himself! Lordy, that's the best I've felt since I don't know when!"

"But it ain't fair!" said Della. "A woman can't make it without a husband! She can barely get by and that's about it. She'll never have anything . . . she'll never be able to afford her own home."

"Says who?" retorted Beatrice. "Why do ya need a man, you're sittin' on a gold mine."

"A gold mine?" said Della. "Ain't nobody in my family owns any property, leastways a gold mine."

"That ain't what I mean, *Miss Podunk,* you *are* the gold

mine, at least the part you're sittin' on. That's what they're all after and they'll pay dearly for it."

"You don't mean . . ."

"That's exactly what I mean. Just think about it. You been raised to think you can't take money for your lovin' but what do you think you're doing when you get married? He pays out money for you a place to live, he pays out money for your food, he pays out money for everything just so's he can have it anytime he wants it, and if that ain't sellin' it, then I don't know what is."

"No, that's not right!" said Della, "It doesn't make you a whore just because you let him have it any time he wants, for god's sake! That's what you're supposed to do, he's your husband!"

"No honey, that doesn't make you a whore, the whore's the one he'll run off with when your butt gets wide and your tits start to sag. He'll leave you having to work someplace like this shit-hole, just so you can get by, and he won't give it a second thought. Trust me, when the new wears off, he'll get all horny and move on to something new, something *strange*, I think is what men call it. So tell me again that ain't sellin' it!"

"Did you ever . . . you know, did you . . .?"

"Did I ever take money for it?" Beatrice asked. "I thought about it a couple times, but that's as far as it went."

"I don't know," said Della. "I don't think I could ever bring myself to take money for, you know, to let somebody . . . "

"Well of course not honey, you'd rather keep on giving it away just like the rest of us. You let ole Ern have all he wanted for free, didn't you? I don't mean to make light of it honey-bunny, but that's the truth. And if that hurts your feelins', I'm sorry."

"You think maybe you could've done that for a living if you didn't have your son? I mean, you couldn't be a prostitute and raise a kid."

"Pauline did!"

"Who's Pauline?"

"Pauline . . .Tabor, I think her name is. She runs Pauline's and I hear she's got two sons, though she more'n likely had help raising 'em."

"What's Pauline's?"

"You've never heard of Pauline's? It's probably the most famous whorehouse in the country and it's just up the road in Bowling Green, Kentucky."

Della took Beatrice's words to heart, although her logic went against everything she'd been taught, which was precious little. But it made sense in a twisted kind of way. All she'd known in her young life was poverty and hard work, the same kind of poverty and hard work that drained her mother's joy and left her dangling on the edge of death at the age of sixty-one. And horrible as it was to say, her sisters were facing the same dismal future; they were overweight and unattractive, but more frightening, they were satisfied with their lives just the way they were. But that was their choice, and if they were happy living like that, then so be it, that was their business. But Della soon decided she'd rather die than work in that mill for the rest of her life, or suffer the degradation of a philandering and abusive husband, and if that's all life had to offer, she'd just as soon go on and die now.

Della stepped to the curb just outside the door of the Greyhound station in Bowling Green, Kentucky, and hailed the taxi driver who was sitting in the bright yellow car parked just a few feet away. He took her small cardboard suitcase in one hand and opened the rear door of the cab with the other.

"Where to, Miss?" he said, and when she replied "Six-twenty-seven Clay Street," he took his hand off the meter and turned facing her with his arm stretched across the top of the front seat. He gave her a lurid smile.

"Did I hear you right, young lady? You're going to Pauline's? Don't know why a pretty young girl like yourself would be going there unless . . . oh I'm sorry . . . that's none of my business. I'll be more'n happy to drive you, but it's only a half block down that street right over there. You can't miss it, it's the one with the chain stretched between the posts all around the yard, and if the milk can's on the porch that means she's open for business. But I guess you already know that." Della blushed, then thanked the cabby for his honesty. She slipped a dime into his hand and reached for her suitcase.

A rather hefty, but attractive, lady opened the door and looked Della over from head to toe, then she smiled.

"Well dearie," she said. "I'd say you're either here looking for work or you think that your hubby's in here and you've got all his worldly belongings in that suitcase!"

"Are you Miss Tabor?" Della asked.

"Name's Pauline, honey, and I'm a missus, not a miss."

"Oh, I'm sorry," said Della, "and yes, I guess you could

say I'm here looking for a position." With that, Pauline burst into laughter.

"Well, you've certainly come to the right place, you'll find all the *positions* you want, right here! Come on in darlin' and let's have a talk."

Pauline Tabor looked like anything but a bawdyhouse Madam. To Della, she looked more like somebody's grandmother and reminded her of a picture she'd seen of this dignified old lady on the label of a gin bottle. She was a full bodied woman, she was dressed very nicely and her gray hair was pulled back neatly into a bun. Her demeanor was friendly, and even though she tried to put Della at ease, it was difficult because of her overwhelming presence.

"Have a seat, dear," Pauline said, after leading her into the parlor that was beautifully decorated, except for the bright red Coca-Cola machine.

"Would you like a Coke, honey, or maybe a cup of tea?"

"No, but thank you," said Della. Her mouth was dry as the cotton back in Cash Point and she was terrified. She wasn't afraid of Pauline Tabor so much as it was knowing she was one step away from becoming a . . . she couldn't say the word. She'd been using words like *working girl, professional woman*, even *lady of the evening*, but now the reality of the situation was staring her in the face; she was on the verge of becoming a whore.

"This is a big step, Della." Pauline said frankly. "And I hope you've given it a lot of thought. It's not for everyone. Most girls do it for the money. They'll work for a while to save a nest egg, then go back to wherever they came from and settle down with some ole boy who thinks she's been waitin' tables at some fancy resort where the guests are rich and the tips are outrageous. Then, there are the girls who do it for kicks; they think it's gonna be easy and all fun and games til the first ugly fat guy drops his undies and makes 'em wish they were back home workin' at a Woolworth's, or behind the counter of some corner drug store. I don't know what your reasons are, honey, and I don't need to, but if you're running away from something, this ain't the answer."

"You can call me Pauline," she said, after they came to an agreement. She went over the house rules; the *do's and don'ts* of the flesh business; the benefits as well as the drawbacks.

"You'll have your own room and your meals will be provided. You'll see a doctor once a week to make sure you're disease free and you'll take time off each month during your period."

"Your girls see a doctor every week?" Della asked.
"Wow, that must get expensive!"

"The doc and I have an *arrangement*." Pauline chuckled, then she went over the financial aspects of the job.

"A quickie is five dollars, two of which you keep, and an all-nighter is twenty-five. You're free to negotiate for anything else you're willing to do, and the house gets sixty percent and you keep forty. You look like an honest girl, but I'm gonna tell you anyway; I catch you holding out on me and you'll be out of here before you know it and you'll never work here again, or at any other brothel in this state! That I can guarantee. Now, do you have any questions?"

Pauline called for one of the girls whose name was Lisa, to show Della to her room and go over a few of the basics.

"Your *uniforms* are in the top drawer," Lisa giggled, referring to an ample supply of garter belts and nylons. "And if they're not the right size, we have a good supply downstairs in the linen closet. There's a pan and a pitcher on the bureau and you can get warm water from the bathroom out in the hall. We open at 1:00 p.m. every day and Pauline expects you to be dressed and downstairs by

12:50. If you need anything else, give me a holler, I'm in the next room."

The house at 627 Clay Street was a picturesque early American style, and looked like anything but a brothel. The first floor was comprised by the oversized parlor that contained the Coca-Cola machine and an elegant mahogany bar. There was the kitchen, a dining room with a table that would seat twelve, and in the hallway were *his* and *her's* restrooms. Pauline's private quarters were just off the kitchen and accessible by invitation only. There were six bedrooms upstairs and one bathroom in the hallway that the girls all shared. The house was huge, even though from the outside it looked no bigger than most. An oversized, graveled parking lot covered what would have otherwise been the back yard and the whole place was encircled by a fence made from heavy wooden posts with lengths of chain strung in between. When the house was closed, a length of chain spanned the driveway and a milk can was placed conspicuously in the center. When the house was open for business, the milk can set at the top of the back porch steps .

Lisa and Della were climbing the stairs when Pauline called out,

"Oh, I forgot to tell you Della, tomorrow you're gonna be a virgin, so don't forget in case anybody asks."

"What's that all about?" Della asked.

"Pauline has a few special friends she calls whenever we get a new girl, and she always tells 'em the girl's a virgin. I don't know if they believe her or not, but just say that you are in case he asks. Oh, and by the way, this one will be a freebie."

Della lined up at the foot of the stairway with the other girls at 12:50, just like she'd been told. She was embarrassed standing there in nothing but her panties, a garter belt and hose with her breasts fully visible through the sheer negligee that hung almost to her spiked heels . . . it was humiliating, she felt cheap . . . she felt like a whore. Shortly after one o'clock, a portly man entered the room from a door somewhere in the back of the house and was personally greeted by Pauline. She led him directly to Della and introduced him as *Burt*. Della could feel her stomach churn when the paunchy, balding man stared at her breasts rather than her face.

"You're right Pauline," he said , drooling like Pavlov's dog. "This-un's a looker!" Then, without asking her name, he said, "Come on sweetheart," and took her by the hand. "Show me which un's your room." He closed the door behind him, unbuckled his gun belt and hung it over the back of the ladder-back chair in the corner. He then took off his brown leather boots, his khaki pants and his shirt, to which was pinned the badge that identified him as Warren County Sheriff. It all made sense. Della closed her eyes when he dropped his baggy boxers . . . she wanted to throw up, but she laid back on the bed, closed her eyes and took a deep breath.

"I know this'll be your first time, honey," said Burt. "So I'll be gentle. Don't be a'scared, ok?"

In just under two minutes, Della's first act as a professional woman was over. She wanted to cry, but told herself it was just a job. Self recrimination was pointless. It wasn't good like it was with Ernie, but she'd been in love with Ernie, and besides, they'd always done it in the dark. Burt dressed himself, winked at her and left the room. She poured warm water from the pitcher into the pan, washed herself and got dressed, such as it was, and when she headed down the stairs she was greeted by applause and uproarious laughter from the other girls, Pauline included. She was now official.

It was shortly after eleven that night when Della went to bed alone, having entertained three men, in addition to the sheriff, two of whom appeared to be college students. She had earned a total of six dollars that day for just over one hour's work. Lying alone in the darkness, she calculated that it would have taken fifteen grueling hours at the mill for her to have made six dollars. She smiled.

She hadn't had to listen to any bullshit, she hadn't had to tell anybody she loved them, or that she even liked them, and she hadn't had to kiss a single one of them.

Della and the other girls soon became friends. Lisa, whom she'd met on her first day there, was a sultry thirty-year-old who had been with Pauline for almost five years. Shirley was a quiet, pretty girl from Paducah who sent money home each week to help her family who'd lost their home in a spring flood and were struggling to get back on their feet. Then there was Jonquil.

Jonquil was a very pretty girl who called herself a *Creole* and claimed to be from New Orleans, but she spoke with a heavy northeastern accent. Della had to take Pauline's word about the accent because she'd never been around any northerners, but she could hear a difference in Jonquil's accent and the way she pronounced certain words. Pauline told her in private that, more than likely, Jonquil was Puerto Rican and was from New York City. But regardless of where she was from, she was Pauline's top money maker. She was slightly on the pudgy side, had gigantic breasts and more repeat customers than all the other girls combined. Jillian, a student at Western Kentucky State College was working on her teaching degree, and lastly, Mary Margaret was a recent divorcee from over near Hopkinsville. Della got along well with all the girls, except for Jonquil whom she hardly knew and seldom saw because she was either busy with customers or asleep on the sofa. She discovered that they were all regular girls just like herself and that they were all in it for the money.

"You'll get used to it," Mary Margaret told her "You just have to look at it as a job. Most of the customers are ok, they're just looking for something they can't get anywhere else."

Things didn't usually get busy on weekdays until after five o'clock, leaving lots of time for the girls to read or play pinochle with Pauline at the big dining room table. Pauline was plenty capable of dealing with unruly customers, though she claimed she hadn't had one in years. She made sure everyone knew she kept a loaded shotgun behind the kitchen door and a .32 caliber revolver in a nearby drawer. She was affable and required nothing of any visitor other than at the very least, they buy a Coca-Cola from her big red machine.

"It helps with the overhead," she'd tell them with a chuckle, but she meant it. Of course that didn't apply to the ones who paid to go upstairs for a frolic with one of her beauties. She loved to play cards and would take on anyone, from her girls who weren't currently entertaining customers to those who were simply waiting for a friend. And should anyone balk at the price of a Coke, she would jokingly rake them over the coals.

"It's only a nickel, for Christ's sake!" she would harangue an unsuspecting guest. "Surely you can afford a nickel! Tell me you can't come up with a nickel and I'll open the machine and give you one on the house!" To date, she'd had only one taker.

Pauline's most strict and staunchly enforced rule was that nobody, but *nobody,* was allowed to go upstairs if they'd had too much to drink. Cocktails and beer were available at the bar and provided a handsome profit, but all customers were advised to belly up *after* they'd finished with their upstairs business.

"Drink up, boys!" Pauline would say. "But don't overdo it if you're planning to party!"

Della had been at Pauline's for just over two months when late on a Saturday afternoon, two college students who'd just come from an Austin Peay-Western Kentucky football game came in for a little romance. One of them took Della's hand and headed for the stairway, but tripped on the first step and almost fell.

"Whoa cowboy!" Pauline called out to the obviously inebriated youngster. "You come back here and let me have a look at your eyes." The boy turned and weaved his way back to where she was standing.

"Sorry, buddy boy," she said. "You ain't going nowhere, you're drunk!"

"But I only had two beers," he told her, "and I can't even feel it."

"I don't care if you only had a thimble-full," she said, "you're drunk, so you're gonna have to sit this one out! That's the rule and there are no exceptions. Here," she said, "let me buy you a Coke and you can take a seat over there and at least look at the girls while you wait for your buddy." She dropped a nickel into the slot, flipped off the cap and handed him the icy bottle. Then she let out a boisterous laugh and patted his shoulder. "Be sure and tell all your friends back in Clarksville that old Pauline, herself, bought you an ice-cold Coca-Cola! And listen son, you're always welcome here, so the next time you plan a trip to Bowling Green, please come by and see us, but drink a Coke before you get here and save the alcohol for later!"

The heartbroken lad settled onto the sofa with his Coke and stared at the girls' boobs while his friend attempted to come to his defense.

"If you don't mind my asking, ma'am, why can't he go

upstairs?" Pauline turned to the boy and took a hard look into *his* eyes, just to be sure he was sober.

"Here's what happens," she began. "First of all, he'll get upstairs and can't get it up because he's had too much to drink. Then, because he can't get it up, he'll want his money back and when he doesn't get his money back he'll want to fight about it. Our policy *is,* we do *not* give refunds and we don't *tolerate* fighting so that's why we have that rule!"

"I get that," he said, "but my buddy here's peaceful as a lamb and I assure you he would never start any trouble." Pauline leaned forward and glared onto the boy's eyes.

"How do you know son, did you ever try to screw him?"

Della's monthly *medical leave* came during the week of her first Christmas at Pauline's, and with her purse full of more cash than she'd seen in her whole life, she went shopping and splurged on gifts for her mother and sisters. She caught a Greyhound to Nashville and then took a city bus to their home on Louisiana Avenue in *The Nations*. It was almost a year since she'd left Nashville and she was shocked and saddened by her mother's appearance . . . Inez was dying. Maureen and Nora had both gained weight and seemed to enjoy spending their time bickering over household finances, the nightly menu or anything else they could think of to argue about. They made Della's visit miserable . . . no matter the subject, they fought about it. The sisters all complimented Della on her nice clothes and how good she looked, but Nora continuously questioned how she'd managed to land such a lucrative bank job in a town so far away, having only a seventh-grade education.

Back in Bowling Green, things were hopping. The war was over, and night after night, boys from Camp Campbell formed a line that extended from the bottom of the stairway, past the Coca-Cola machine and out onto the porch. The girls were having a devil of a time keeping up, but were making more money than they could count as they welcomed the strong and handsome young men who were a sight for sore eyes compared to the older, pot-bellied regulars.

Della was headed down the stairway on a busy Saturday night after having finished with her eighth customer of the day, then stopped short on the bottom step when she heard a familiar voice. She peeked around the corner to see her worst nightmare standing less than six feet away; it was her brother, Martin. His back was to her and he was chatting with another sailor while patiently awaiting his turn. She made her way into the kitchen and waved to Pauline to get her attention.

"My brother's standing out there by the stairs!" she said in a near panic. "He's one of those two sailors over by the Coke machine, the one on the left. I can't let him see me, Pauline, I just can't!" She was almost in tears. "I know we're busy, but please don't make me go back out there!" Pauline stepped into the parlor to check out the young man, then came back into the kitchen and rolled her eyes in approval.

"He's pretty cute!" she teased. "I've always had a thing for sailor-boys, I might just take him on, myself!" Then she pulled Della close and hugged her. "You go on back to my room and stay there til I come and get you, honey. It won't be long," she laughed. "He's the next one in line and if he's like all the rest, he'll be out of here in less than fifteen minutes."

It was on a Saturday afternoon in early spring that Della was picked from the line by a gentleman who appeared to be a cut above the usual *John*. He was well dressed, looked to be in his early forties and was just over six feet tall, maybe six-one. He was a trim one-hundred seventy pounds, had graying temples and was extremely handsome. His eyes moved slowly from one girl to the next, then stopped when he saw Della. All of Pauline's girls were beautiful, but there was something different about Della. She didn't display herself like the others, she looked more like a timid bride on her wedding night, allowing her groom to see her body for the first time. She took his hand and led him up the steps to her room where she learned that his name was Alan; only first names were used at Pauline's. When she finished examining and washing him, he pulled her to his chest, bare skin on bare skin, and kissed her. There is an unwritten rule that kissing is excluded from a prostitute's list of services, but in Alan's case, Della chose to ignore it. When they finished, he paid her for a second go-round, which of course lasted considerably longer than the first. Of all the men who frequented Pauline's, Alan was the first one that Della found pleasurable.

On the Saturday afternoon exactly two weeks after Della first met Alan, he showed up again, and this time he asked for her by name. He paid for the remainder of her day, as well as the entire night.

"How bout we get dressed and go somewhere nice for dinner," he said after their second session.

"Dinner? You want to take me to dinner? I don't know if Pauline will let me," she said. "She doesn't allow us to leave the house during working hours."

"Well," he said. "I'm paid up until eight o'clock tomorrow morning and it seems to me if I want to take you to dinner, I should be allowed. But if you'd like, I'll go ask for her permission."

The waiter set two wine glasses onto the table and filled them from the bottle Alan had brought with him. Dining establishments in Warren County, along with most other counties in Kentucky, were prohibited by law from selling alcohol, but customers were allowed to bring their own bottle. Della had never seen such elegant surroundings, and in fact had never even eaten in a restaurant, except for the lunch counter at the Nashville Greyhound Station where she'd tasted her first hamburger. She stared at the menu not knowing what many of the items were, and with disbelief at the prices.

"See anything you like?" Alan asked as he placed his hand over hers. "Please order anything you want."

Della was out of her element and was intimidated by just being there. She only knew Alan slightly from their first date two weeks prior and was puzzled why he would spend his time or money bringing her to a place like this. It was a hard and fast rule at Pauline's that you don't ask personal questions, but considering the circumstances . . .

"Why did you bring me here?" she asked.

"Because I wanted to," he said. "It seemed like a good

idea, and besides, I'm hungry, aren't you? Speaking of which, where and when do you usually have dinner?"

"Pauline keeps lunchmeat in the refrigerator and we grab a quick sandwich when things slow down, but on most nights, especially Saturdays, we're lucky if we get anything until well after midnight." She slowly looked around, wondering if any of the men in the room recognized her.

"I assume you're not from Bowling Green," she said, "else you wouldn't take me out in public."

"You're right, I'm not from Bowling Green, but it wouldn't matter . . . I'd take you into any restaurant back at home. And to answer your question about why I brought you here, I get lonely. It's not all about the sex, I need female companionship; someone to talk to. I get tired of eating alone."

"So, you're not married?"

"No, I'm a widower. My wife died just over a year ago. I know several ladies who are available, but right now there's nobody I'm interested in." Then he shrugged and said with a smile. "They don't make any bones about the fact they're looking for a husband, and a couple of 'em are fairly good looking, but the spark just isn't there. It's obvious they're just looking for somebody with a little money to take care of them and . . . oh, you don't want to hear all that." He shifted the conversation to more lightweight small talk. They finished dinner and returned to Della's room where they made love one more time and then slept until 7:30 the next morning.

Della was familiar with the *man-on-top* kind of sex and its accompanying variations, but prior to coming to Pauline's, she had no concept of the perversion that lurks in the minds of some people. She knew there were men who like men and women who like women, but she had no idea there were people who got their jollies from physical pain, as well as from inflicting pain onto others. Lisa informed her late on a Wednesday afternoon that the house would be closed that evening from seven until eight because one of Pauline's *high-rollers* was coming in for his *special session* and she always shut the place down because of the screaming and excessive noise that she didn't want her other clients to hear. Della listened, her mouth agape and her eyes open wide as Lisa described what was going to take place.

"The trick is a big-wig in state politics," Lisa told her, "and according to Pauline, he's been coming here for years. I don't know how much he pays her, but it must be a lot if she can afford to shut the place down for a whole hour. He pays her to provide him with two girls dressed in black leather to whip him. It's really freaky and I don't get it, but for the fifty dollars Pauline pays me, I'll beat on him all night long, no questions asked. He gets off on hurting others as well as being hurt so we tie him face down on the bed so he doesn't get carried away and try to hurt one of us. When we finish, he's got these big, bloody welts all over his backside, and we have to wash him with cold water and then rub him down with salve. Like I said, he's a real sicko but the money's good. Anyway, do you wanna make fifty bucks tonight?" Della thought it over and came to the decision that for fifty dollars she'd join in. And, she was curious to learn the identity of *Mister Big Shot*.

Just after seven that evening the mysterious customer arrived and was introduced by Pauline simply as *Simon*. She stayed in Lisa's room until he was fully naked and lying face down on the bed with his wrists and ankles tied securely.

"Knock yourselves out, ladies," Pauline said with a wink as she headed for the door, "Simon says he's ready!"

Della stood frozen in place, unsure of what to do when suddenly and without notice, Lisa lashed Simon's backside with the strands of braided nylon leaving raw, bloody welts and causing him to cry out in pain.

"What are you waiting for?" Lisa asked impatiently. "Don't just stand there, draw some blood!" Della struck Simon with the whip, first halfheartedly then with greater rapidity and intensity until Lisa had to shout at her to back off.

"Not that rough!" she said. "You don't want to kill him!" She mistakenly thought that Della was enjoying herself and getting into the sadistic savagery, when in fact she was letting out the anger that was built up inside her; she was thrashing her brothers, she was whipping Ernie, she was leaving bloody stripes on Billy Caudill as well as every other customer who'd ever come into her bedroom wearing a wedding band. And so what if Simon, or whatever his name was, was getting his kicks from it, she was giving him the beating he deserved for being so disgusting and because he too, was wearing a wedding ring. Never again was Della asked to participate in any sadomasochistic parties, nor did she want to.

Della eventually became callous to sex with strangers, and like the others, she learned to fake her way through it making the John feel like he wasn't a loser; that's what she was paid to do, make the customer happy. But in the process she concluded that being a prostitute was robbing her of a normal, pleasurable love life. Making love with Alan felt right. It felt like it was supposed to, at least to the best of her knowledge, but she only saw him on alternate Saturdays. He was gentle and considerate, not like any other man she'd ever met. Of all the men she'd encountered, not one had ever asked her to teach him how to please a woman because they obviously didn't care. Alan didn't ask either, but then, he didn't need to.

Della had no illusions of permanency with Alan because he was a gentleman and she *was* a prostitute . . . she accepted that. She allowed herself no false hope, but lying in his arms left her feeling safe and loved until reality slapped her in the face on Sunday mornings when he'd get dressed and head for home. Alan was a *trick* and she knew that's all he would ever be. She knew better than to fall in love with a man whose last name she didn't even know, but despite her best efforts that is exactly what she did.

It all came to an end one Sunday morning when Alan was dressed and ready to leave. He drew her close and kissed her, then told her he wouldn't be coming back.

"I've met a lady I think I can be happy with, so I guess this is goodbye." She hugged him and wished him the best, and she managed to hold back her tears until he was in his car and out of sight.

The possibility of contracting a venereal disease was a

real, though not an insurmountable threat. The doctor successfully taught Pauline's girls how to examine clients for signs of venereal disease prior to engaging in the act, but even if an infected *John* slipped by undetected, with a simple shot of penicillin and a three-day furlough, the problem was solved. According to Pauline, she'd had only three girls come down with gonorrhea or syphilis since she'd opened her first bordello in 1933, attesting to the effectiveness of examining clients as a preventative.

The more likely threat was of becoming pregnant. An unwanted pregnancy had the potential of putting an end to a professional girl's career, and was a surefire way to bring shame onto her family when she showed up at home in a motherly way, unaccompanied by the expectant father. And what would she tell the child someday when questions would undoubtably arise? The alternative would an abortion, performed free of charge by the same doctor who saw to their sexual health. But to most of Pauline's girls, abortion was unacceptable. Whores though they were, they had hearts, and to each, the thought of killing one's own child was abhorrent and out of the question.

Most of the girls, as best they could, practiced the rhythm method that was taught them by the two Roman Catholic priests who were regulars at Pauline's. The horny padres had made the first of their semi-annual trips from Louisville a few years earlier and they always stayed three to four days at a stretch, each one making love to every girl in the house at least once. Upon learning they were priests, Pauline asked them, point-blank, how they could justify breaking their vows of celibacy and still call themselves men of God.

"The flesh is weak," replied the one who called himself Father Timothy. "And I am but flesh, therefore I am weak."

"But don't you Catholics have to go to confession?"

"Ah, yes!" responded the other one, Father Michael. "Ours is a loving God and we receive His forgiveness through confession of our sins." Pauline remained silent for a moment, thoughtfully considering his words.

"But what about your superiors? I don't mean to sound judgmental, it's your religion, not mine, but I wouldn't think you'd be allowed to have sex, especially with prostitutes, and still be priests. How do you get away with it? Doesn't your Bishop, or whoever hears your confession, demand that you either remain celibate or leave the priesthood?" Father Timothy blushed, and then looked ashamedly at Pauline.

"Well," he said. "The Monsignor doesn't hear our

confession so he doesn't know about this. And you're probably right, he'd most likely throw us both out if he did. We are required to confess our sins to an ordained priest, which of course we both are, so we hear one another's confession during the train ride back to Louisville."

After three years at Pauline's, Della was becoming sick of sex with strangers, and after an incredibly busy weekend, she decided it was time to move on. Shortly after her arrival at Pauline's, she began to dream of opening her own place someday and she started watching Pauline closely; how she conducted herself and how she dealt with not only her girls, but with customers as well. She learned things she would have otherwise never known. Pauline Tabor ran a first rate bordello, undoubtedly the finest in Kentucky and perhaps the whole country, and in doing so, she unwittingly became Della's mentor. Della had decided that Nashville would be an ideal place for her new business because it was a busy and growing city with unlimited potential. She sat down with Pauline over coffee one Monday morning and revealed her plans in an open and honest manner.

"I'm sorry to be losing you, Della," said Pauline. "You're one of the best girls I've ever had work for me, and I guess I knew I couldn't hang on to you forever. I want you to know that I mean it when I wish you the best, I really do. And I want you to know that if things don't work out, you'll always have a home right here with me. Listen," she then said. "Always protect the ones who protect you. Make friends with all the politicians and cops you can, and never, ever divulge their names to anyone, regardless of how rough things get. They have to know they can trust you." Then she became teary-eyed when she hugged Della and told her goodbye.

During her years at Pauline's, Della accumulated almost seven-thousand dollars in savings, which in 1950 was a huge sum of money. Before leaving Bowling Green, one of other girls who owned an automobile taught Della to drive, and then one morning during her *medical leave,* she chauffeured Della to Nashville to take the exam to obtain a Tennessee driver's license. The very next morning Della walked to a dealership a few blocks from Pauline's and paid cash for a used, 1949 Ford coupe. She packed all her worldly possessions, said her goodbyes and drove to Nashville where she moved in with her sisters.

Inez was gone now and Maureen still worked at the shirt factory. Francine was an LPN and worked in the nursery at Saint Thomas Hospital while Nora took care of the housekeeping and cooking. Her sisters welcomed her with open arms, as well as open hands, grateful for the money she paid them for room and board. Maureen was sweet, Nora was irritable and demanding and Francine was indifferent, and even though they were family, Della was uncomfortable . . . she felt like an intruder. All three were still curious about her purported job in Bowling Green and skeptical of how she'd managed to buy her own car when it was all they could do to scrape together bus fare.

Della stayed with her sisters for a total of three weeks, which proved to be two and a half weeks too many. She spent days combing the classifieds until she found a suitable rental across the river in East Nashville. She proudly announced to her sisters during supper that evening that she was moving to Lebanon, Tennessee, where she had accepted a job as a branch manager with the Wilson County Bank, when in fact she was moving into a rental house on Fatherland Street in the Edgefield community on the east side of the Cumberland River. Edgefield had been an independent city until it merged with Nashville in 1869, and still reflected much of the opulence of the nineteenth century. The neighborhood was once home to many of the city's elite, but most of the once elegant homes had seen better days. As had the neighborhood, most of them had deteriorated into a state of disrepair. Many were filled with undesirables whose very presence drove down property values and helped drive the area farther into ruin. Della easily saw the potential of the old homes, however, and decided that buying one of them was a risk worth taking.

The former elegance of the abandoned old home caught Della's eye before she noticed the sign in the front yard. She walked into the yard for a closer look and learned that the property had been seized for back taxes and would be sold at auction on the courthouse steps a week from the following Wednesday. The house needed repair, but its potential was unlimited. The roof needed work, some of the exterior trim was missing and of course it needed paint, but the wraparound porch and the stained glass front door made the place impossible to ignore. The front door was locked, but from what she could see through a window that hadn't been washed in years, the interior appeared to be sound. The sign stated that it would be open for inspection from noon until five o'clock on the day before the auction.

Della was there and waiting when a deputy from the Davidson County Sheriff's Office arrived to unlock the front door. He did a double take when he saw Della.

"Don't I know you?" he asked. "You look awfully familiar." He looked familiar to her as well, but she simply said, "I'm sure we've never met, I just moved here from California." He stared at her for another moment and then shrugged. "Guess not," he said and proceeded to unlock the door.

The house had no electricity, and even though the windows were dirty, the natural sunlight proved sufficient. The foyer opened up into the parlor on the right and a grand stairway lay straight ahead. Hanging from the ceiling was a gorgeous old chandelier that was covered in cobwebs and some of the little crystal doodads were missing, but it spoke to the glory of the once elegant home.

"You folks make yourselves at home," said the deputy. "Take your time cause the place will be open until five o'clock."

Besides Della, there were four men and two couples there to inspect the house. One of the men nodded to Della and smiled.

"If you don't mind my asking," he said. "What are your plans for this place if you buy it?" Then he offered his hand and said, "My name is Jeffrey Coulter and I'm a general contractor." He handed her his business card.

"My name is Della Borden and I'm looking for a place to establish a home for wayward girls."

"A home for wayward girls?" he said. His expression reflecting no glimmer of comprehension. "What do you mean by wayward? I mean, what is it you do?"

"This will be a place for girls who've grown up in poverty just like I did. It will be for girls who have little or no education and no direction in life. Hopefully, they'll be able to come here and learn how to make their own way."

"My," he said, "what an admirable goal!"

"What will you do with it?" Della asked.

"Oh, I'll renovate it and put it up for sale," he said. "That's what I do, but I'll have to be careful not to sink so much into it that I can't turn a profit."

"Tell me," she asked. "What will it take to restore this place and how much will it be worth when it's all finished?"

"That's hard to say. The trouble with this place is that it was once a boarding house and there are six large bedrooms upstairs and two downstairs. Nobody wants an eight bedroom house so I'll have to figure a way to convert part of the upstairs to make it more attractive for an average-size family. But six bedrooms would work well for you and your girls, wouldn't it?" he asked.

"It would," she said," and ten would be even better. If I should decide to buy the place, could you make the conversion? And can you give me an estimate of what it will take to renovate this place and what it'll be worth when you're finished?"

"Well, off the top of my head I'll say it will bring somewhere between ten and twelve-thousand and it's gonna take at least seventy-five hundred or eight thousand to get it there. So I'd say right now it's worth fifteen-hundred, two-thousand, tops, and that's not leaving much room for a profit. But I'll tell you what," he said. "If you buy the place, I'd appreciate a chance to bid on the work."

"Well, Mister Coulter," she said, "if I end up with this place, we might just be able to do business."

At precisely 10:00 a.m. on Wednesday, July 18, Della, Jeffrey Coulter, along with five other interested parties, gathered on the steps of the Davidson County Courthouse. A representative from the Sheriff's office had set up a table where potential buyers could register and show proof of their ability to pay. Della added her name to the list, then opened her purse and showed the clerk a wad of cash. He in turn, handed her a card bearing a number, and when the others had all registered, the sheriff announced that the bidding would begin upon the arrival of Probate Judge William McMasters.

Della and Coulter were chatting when out of the corner of her eye she saw a tall, handsomely dressed man emerge from the courthouse door and head toward the place where they were standing. It was Alan! Her heart leapt into her throat, seeing him for the first time in over a year, and as was her habit back at the cotton mill, she looked at his left hand to see if he was married. It hurt a bit when she saw the gold ring, but she was thrilled to see him, nevertheless. He had just stepped up to the table to explain the bidding process when his eyes locked onto hers. For an instant his face went blank . . . he lost his train of thought and appeared to forget why he was even there. Della saw the look of panic in his eyes and flashed a quick smile and an almost imperceptible shake of her head to let him know that his secret was safe. Somehow, he seemed to understand and quickly gathered his composure. He finished with the instructions and opened the floor for bids.

"One thousand dollars!" Coulter shouted.

"Eleven hundred," Della countered. A man in the crowd called out a bid of eleven-hundred and fifty, to which Coulter responded. "twelve-hundred!"

"Twelve-fifty!" shouted Della. The stranger quickly followed with a bid of thirteen-hundred. The action slowed a bit when Coulter bid fourteen-hundred, and when Della raised it to fifteen, the other bidder turned and walked away. Coulter remained in the running until Della's bid went to seventeen-hundred and fifty dollars.

"You are intent on buying this place, aren't you!" to which Della nodded yes, her expression confirming her determination.

"Then I'm bailing out, but remember your promise to let me bid on the renovation."

"Done!" she said, as they smiled and shook hands.

"Going once for seventeen, fifty!" cried the auctioneer. "Twice . . . three times and sold to the young lady for seventeen-hundred, fifty dollars! "Congratulations, Miss," he said. "Now if you will accompany Judge McMasters to the probate office, he will complete the paperwork and give you the deed and the keys."

"You're the last person on earth I expected to see!" said McMasters after closing the office door behind them.

"Same here," said Della. "So what do I call you, William? Bill? Your Honor?"

"Bill will do. Listen Della, I'm married now and . . . "

"Shhhh." she said. "You have nothing to fear from me. I'm happy for you and I would never do anything to embarrass or hurt you, I hope you know that."

"Thank you," he said with a sigh. "You could've knocked me over with a feather when I saw you out there. What are you going to do with that place, are you planning to live there?"

"Yes," she said. "I'll definitely be living there."

"You're not planning to open a . . . well, you know. I don't mean to meddle, but are you going to open . . . "

"A whorehouse?" she said. "Well, I don't know as I should answer that, you being a judge and all."

"Forget I asked," he said. "I don't wanna know. But I promise I won't cause you any trouble, whatever you decide to do."

On the following Monday, Della met with Jeffrey Coulter at her house on Russell Street to discuss plans for the renovation. Downstairs was the parlor, a formal dining room and a large kitchen that featured a walk-in pantry. There was a master bedroom with its own bath, a second bedroom and another bathroom in the hallway. A screened-in porch ran the entire width of the back of the house and overlooked a large, tree covered back yard that was overgrown with saplings and weeds. Upstairs were six bedrooms, but there was only one bathroom in the hallway. Parking was limited to no more than three cars in the short driveway beside the house, but across the back alley was a Kroger's that had a huge parking lot that hadn't gone unnoticed when Della first looked at the property.

"These walls are plaster," said Jeff. "And they'll have to be torn out in order to replace the wiring and plumbing, but we'll go back with gypsum drywall that everybody's using now because it's easier than plaster and a whole lot cheaper to install. I'll need to rewire the place and put in a new heating system and ductwork, and while we're at it, I'll go ahead and run telephone lines. Now, what else did you have in mind?"

"Can you convert the six upstairs bedrooms to eight, like we talked about and maybe put in a couple more bathrooms so the girls can have more privacy?"

"Of course I can," said Coulter, thinking it a bit extravagant for wayward girls who'd likely grown up without indoor plumbing. But that was none of his business, and accordingly, he offered no comment.

"And of course it needs a new roof," he added, "and some of the outside trim needs to be replaced and the whole house needs to be painted. Hav you decided the color you'd like on the outside?"

"White, of course!" beamed Della. "It has to be white!"

It was just after 3:00 p.m. and the morning shift people were streaming out the doors of the cotton mill like the place was on fire. Della was sitting in her car, watching for Beatrice, and when she saw her crossing the street. She tapped the car horn and called out her name. Bea put her hand over her eyes to block the glare and flashed that gorgeous smile of hers when she saw it was Della.

"Lordy girl, just look at you! And where did you steal this car?"

"Get in," said Della, "I'll drive you home . . . and I bought this car with my own money, thank you!"

Beatrice had changed very little in the three years since they'd seen one another; her hair was the same gorgeous red, she still had a great body, though perhaps five pounds heavier, and she still had that angelic face.

"God, I've missed you!" said Beatrice as she pulled Della close and hugged her like she used to when they shared lunch on the back steps. "I didn't think I'd ever see you again, how long's it been anyway?"

"A little over three years," said Della, "but it seems

longer." The small talk continued until Beatrice got up the nerve to ask the big question.

"So tell me, what's it like working at Pauline's?"

"It wasn't too bad, once I got the hang of it. Of course most of the customers are losers," she said, "you know, the ones who couldn't get laid on a bet! But most of them don't last over a couple of minutes so you just close your eyes and groan like you're enjoying it. Their money's as good as the cute ones' though, and they don't mind turning it loose. Besides, most of the money you make is from losers anyhow, because the good looking ones have other options.

Anyway, I've had all of that I want. I just quit Pauline's and moved back to Nashville. You know, I learned a lot from Pauline, the main thing being that she's got the right idea; she doesn't lie down for anybody and she spends most of her time shootin' the breeze with customers, playing cards and counting her money."

"So what are you gonna do, are you thinking about opening a place of your own?"

"That's exactly what I'm gonna to do, and I want you to come in with me. I've already got the house. It needs a lot of work, but it should be ready in a couple or three months."

"You want me to go into it with you? Honey, I'm too old for all that, and besides I don't know if I'm cut out for . . . well, you know."

"I'm not talking about turning tricks," said Della. "I want you to help me run the place, I want you to be my partner. It's gonna be a seven-day a week operation and I can't do it by myself. Besides, you're a long way from being too old, honey," she said. "You're still prettier than most of the girls who'll be working there, and besides, you'll be in charge so you can do anything you want . . . like maybe if you get to feeling a little frisky? Trust me honey, there are boatloads of guys out there who'd pay good money for a roll in the hay with you!"

"Oh hush!" said Bea. Her face now red as her hair. "Do you really think so?"

Della met again with Jeff Coulter the following week to go over the details of his estimate.

"What's the bad news?" she asked.

"Well, I've gone over everything we talked about and I came up with a price of eighty-three-hundred dollars, give or take, to make this place look brand new."

"Does that include the changes to the upstairs we talked about?"

"It includes everything. Here, I made you an itemized copy in case you wanna make changes." She studied the list then folded it and stuck it into her purse.

"I'll need a few days to raise the money," she said, trying to calculate in her head how much it would take to get the place furnished and decorated. She'd left Pauline's with almost seven-thousand dollars, from which she paid seventeen-hundred and fifty for the house, leaving her with a little over five thousand. Knowing it would take most of that to furnish the house, she realized that she'd need to borrow enough money to pay for the renovation.

"You do this for a living," she said to Jeff, "so tell me where I can get a mortgage loan?" On the back of his business card, he wrote the name of a Mister Gibson at the West Nashville Branch of Third National Bank on Charlotte Avenue in West Nashville.

"This man's your best bet," said Coulter. "He's helped a lot of people get businesses up and running, including mine, so be sure and tell him I'll be doing the work."

"What are your plans for the place?" asked Andy Gibson, branch manager and Senior Vice President of Third National Bank, one of Nashville's *big three*. "Is it going to be your residence?"

"Yes, it will, but I'll be running a business from there as well."

"And what kind of business is that?"

"Temporary help," she answered. "There's a big demand for girls on a short-term basis."

"Hmmm," said Gibson, "I haven't heard of that one, but it sounds like a good idea. You may be on to something." He leaned back and crossed one leg over the other and stared out the window, chewing on a cigar stub and appearing to not be listening as Della laid out her plan. She was discouraged and about to pick up her papers and walk out when Gibson turned and opened his desk drawer, pulled out a loan application and slid it across the desk.

"Fill that out and sign it, and leave it and Coulter's bid with me," he said, "along with the deed and I'll get an appraiser over there to check it out. I don't see a problem, but check back with me in three or four days. We'll get this ball rolling."

Della wrapped a silk scarf around her face like she used to do at the cotton mill, but instead of lint, it was to keep from breathing the dust created by the plaster being ripped from the walls. She tried to not be a nuisance, but every couple or three days she couldn't resist driving over to Russell Street to check on the progress.

"We'll have her gutted by tomorrow," said Jeff. "Then you'll really start to see the changes when we start putting it all back together."

The piles of rubble in the yard were soon hauled away and replaced with stacks of new lumber that shrank each day as the interior began to take shape. The former elegance slowly began to reappear as the walls went up and each piece of the original moulding was stripped of the old paint and carefully nailed back into place. The grand stairway was sanded and ready to be varnished when Della climbed the steps to inspect the upstairs bedrooms. Everything was taking shape and showing the promise of a return to its former elegance, the masterpiece being the crystal chandelier that had been rewired, polished and hung back into its place of prominence in the foyer.

Watching the interior come together was more than exciting for Della, but she could hardly contain herself the day she parked at the curb and saw the painters hard at work. More than half the front was covered in breathtaking white and it was gorgeous! It was only the primer coat, but it was far more beautiful than she'd imagined. The wide boards on the front porch had been replaced and were ready to be covered with two coats of gray, and the bead-board ceiling was already painted back to its original *sky-blue*.

"Give me three more weeks and you'll be ready to move in." Jeff told Della. It was almost Christmas and the weather had cooperated and allowed the work to progress rapidly and without a hitch.

"Are you happy with everything?" asked Coulter Though Della had a hard time finding the words, her smile told him that the big white house on Russell Street was more magnificent than she'd ever imagined.

"You know," he said, "if I'd known this place was gonna turn out so well, I'd probably have kept on bidding. I feel comfortable saying this house is worth a minimum of fourteen thousand right now, and maybe more. And I don't mind telling you, I'm very proud of the way it turned out, and I would appreciate it if you tell everybody it was my company that did the work."

Della picked Beatrice up on a bright, cold Sunday morning and drove to East Nashville to show her the house.

"My God!" said Beatrice when she saw it. "Is this it? My lord, It's gorgeous! It's the most beautiful house I've ever seen!"

On the wrap-around porch was an assortment of wicker furniture, and there was a beautiful old swing that was hung from the ceiling around on the side. The stained glass in the front door took Bea's breath, then seeing the chandelier in the foyer almost finished her off. The newly refinished hardwood floors were breathtaking, as was the oriental rug in the parlor. As the tour progressed, Beatrice's disbelief grew and she was awestruck by the huge kitchen and the one-time back porch that was now closed in and boasted a bar that was half the length of the room.

"Are you going to serve alcohol?" Bea asked.

"Absolutely," said Della. "There's a lot of money in booze, but I've got to find a bartender who can double as a bouncer."

"Are you expecting trouble?" asked Bea.

"Not if I find the right bartender." Della answered with a smile. "Pauline maintained a bar from the day she opened her first brothel and says she's never had a problem. But of course, everyone knew she kept a shotgun and a pistol handy."

Della's private bedroom was in the back corner of the house and the other downstairs bedroom was just across the hall.

"Will this room be used by one of your girls?" asked Beatrice.

"No," said Della. "Customers will only be entertained upstairs."

"Then what is this, a spare bedroom?"

"No," said Della. "It'll be your room if you want it. Like I told you honey, I'm gonna need help running this place and I was serious when I asked you to be my partner. I can't think of anybody I'd rather partner-up with than you! I'm serious, Bea, let's talk about it. I can't have you coming into this with a blind eye. I want you to know that there is always a risk of being arrested. I don't think either one of us would ever face any serious jail time, but your picture might wind up in the newspaper and probably on television as well. You need to decide which is more important, your reputation or the money. And then there's Denny. He can't live here and I also know that he is the most important person in your life, so I'll understand if you say no."

"It's funny you brought him up," said Bea, "because Denny won't figure into it. When he turned fourteen, he all of a sudden got too big for his britches and he lost control of his tongue. He let out a string of cuss words one night when I got after him for not doing his homework and I busted his lip for him. Of course that just made him madder and he started yelling that he wanted to go live with his daddy! So I handed him the telephone receiver and told him to go for it! Well, he moved in with Donnie Ray a couple months ago and I guess it's working out pretty well for both of 'em, but I admit, I miss him."

Bea sat down on the edge of the bed and bit her lip to keep from crying. She wiped her eyes, and then she began to laugh. It was a chuckle at first, then escalated into a seemingly uncontrollable belly laugh.

"What's so funny?" Della asked.

"Oh, I was just thinking about tomorrow when I go to the mill and tell 'em to kiss my ass!"

"Then it's settled!" shrieked Della. She was actually jumping up and down. "You're really gonna do it? You're gonna move in here with me?"

"Well, yeah I guess, if you really want me to, but I don't know anything about the *whoring* business, what will I be doing?"

"What's to know? You just make sure the girls keep themselves clean and fixed up pretty, and that the customers have a good time. Oh yeah, and you'll see to it that they behave themselves. If they don't, you throw their asses out! You'll be great at it, honey, and like I told you, if you get to feeling a little frisky and wanna do a little entertaining of your own . . . well, that'll be your business."

After years at the cotton mill, Beatrice was making eighty cents an hour, just five cents above minimum wage. Her foreman was visibly shaken when she gave him notice and promised to try and get her a raise if she'd agree to stay.

"You do the work of two people," he said, "and I don't know how I'll ever replace you."

"Then you should have been paying me the wages of two people!" she sneered at him. "You damn people don't deserve good employees because you don't treat 'em right! You suck out their blood and you don't give a shit about any of 'em! It never crossed your mind to give me a raise until I told you I'm ready to walk out the door, and now you wanna get all generous? Well, Joe, it's nothing personal, but you can tell the people who own this place they can take their piddly-ass raise, this shit-hole mill and all their cotton, and shove it!" She then went home and gave notice to her landlord, paid the rent up to date, packed her belongings and moved out the very next morning.

While the construction was ongoing, Della discreetly spread the word that she was looking for girls. Pauline referred a young woman who'd been with her for over a year, but now wanted to leave Bowling Green for personal reasons, and felt that Nashville was as good a place to live as any. She introduced herself as Delilah, although Della doubted that was her real name. It didn't matter, though, lots of prostitutes liked using seductive names, thinking it a turn-on to customers. She met with Della shortly before Christmas and agreed to come to work as soon as the house was ready to open, which was on schedule for late January.

Della spread the word among the bellmen at a few of the better downtown hotels while Beatrice approached some of the younger women she'd known at the cotton mill. Beatrice used vague language when describing the job, figuring that any of the girls who were interested would easily read between the lines. She came away with one very interested candidate, a girl named Billie Jean Hargrove, a perky little brunette who lived in *The Nations* on Pennsylvania Avenue. She worked the day shift at the mill and nights at Redmond's, a local dive where she tended bar and waited tables. Billie Jean was basically a good girl, but she knew her way around. She jumped at the offer when Beatrice promised that she would make ten times more money lying on her back than she could standing on her feet.

Everything was in place. The house was furnished, the bar was stocked and two of the proposed eight girls had already moved in. Della made a deal with a doctor at nearby Miller Clinic to examine the girls every week in exchange for sexual favors. She also passed the word discreetly among several cabbies who passed it on to a couple of deputies in the Davidson County Sheriff's Office that they were welcome to stop by and take their pick of the five young virgins who would be available prior to opening day, but that they'd better not wait too long.

Beatrice hired a bartender who was of sufficient size to double as a bouncer. Barney Willis was a two-hundred, seventy-pound former tackle from Vanderbilt University who'd flunked out of school shortly after the last game of his senior year. He was an affable Teddy Bear with whom all the girls fell in love. They provided benefits that far exceeded Barney's expectations and he charged headlong into his work with the exuberance of a five-year-old on Christmas Eve.

The big day finally came on Saturday, January 27th at 1:00 p.m. when Delilah, Billie Jean and two new girls, Jackie and Louise, donned their *work clothes*, ready for business. Della and Beatrice were decked out in their Sunday best and were anxiously awaiting customers when the first knock came at the door just before dark. Della opened the door to find a couple of smiling ole boys who looked to be in their mid-thirties.

"Are you Della?" One of them asked.

"I sure am!" she answered. "Y'all come on in and make yourselves at home." Words couldn't describe their glee when they walked into the parlor and saw the girls with their assets fully on display.

"How'd y'all hear about us?" asked Della.

"This guy named Joey over at the Peco Truck Stop on North First Street told us," said the one who introduced himself as *Paul*. "We stop there and eat every time we come through Nashville, and if it's on the weekend we usually stay over til Monday. Joey usually fixes us up with a couple lot lizards, but he suggested we drive over here and check out your place, said he heard it was gonna be real nice." Della made a mental note to pay Joey a visit and take him a bottle of Jack Daniels as a way of saying *thank you!* While she was at it, she'd invite him over for a complimentary romp with his choice of the girls. She'd learned from Pauline where to plant seeds and how to cultivate them.

"So you boys are truck drivers," said Bea. "Where 'bouts you from?"

"Louisiana," said Paul. "I'm from Lafayette and *Zeke,* here's from Baton Rouge. He's my co-driver'n his real name's Ezekiel, but I just call him Zeke. Say, do you think our truck'll be all right in that grocery store parking lot across the alley? That's where Joey said we should park, but I can't afford to take no chances, it's a company truck."

"It'll be fine," Beatrice said, flashing her gorgeous smile. "We have an arrangement with the store manager."

Paul and Zeke settled in for the weekend, alternating between trips upstairs and playing pinochle with Della and Beatrice in the dining room. Zeke had been paying special attention to both Della and Beatrice and finally got up the nerve to ask, "How much for you two?" They both burst into laughter and Beatrice replied, "I'm not for hire," and Della said, "and you can't afford me!" Another three customers showed up that later in the evening. One was a traveling salesman referred by a bellman at the Noel Hotel and the other two, both college students, were home for the weekend. All in all, Della felt the turnout was excellent considering it was their first day.

They all gathered for breakfast in the dining room at 9:00

a.m. on Sunday morning, including Paul and Zeke who'd paid thirty dollars each to spend the night. Barney proved to be an excellent cook, and with Beatrice's help, turned out a fine breakfast of bacon, sausage, eggs, biscuits and gravy and a pot of hot coffee.

"Paul," said Della, "tell me what you think of the place. Do you feel like you got your money's worth?"

"Did I ever! Let me tell you, Miss Della, Me'n Zeke get around, as you can well imagine, and we've seen some mighty fine establishments. But I can honestly say this is by far the best . . . uh, the best . . ."

"Whorehouse?" said Della. "It's ok, Paul, you can say whorehouse. That's what it is."

"Well, it's a lot more'n that, Miss Della. It's way out'n front of any whorehouse I ever been to!"

"Then you'll come back," said Della. "And I hope you'll tell all your friends."

"Oh yes ma'am!" said Paul. "You can count on that!"

After breakfast they retired to the parlor where, at Della's request, Zeke brought in wood from the side porch and built a fire in the grand old fireplace, the first it had seen in years. The flames had a mesmerizing effect, and between the fire and the biscuits and gravy, everyone was soon asleep, some on the furniture and some on the floor. It was just after noon when Paul went out to fetch more firewood and came back in and said it was drizzling rain and freezing as soon as it hit the ground. The rain soon turned to sleet that continued throughout the night, and by morning everything was covered with almost an inch of solid ice. that broke down power lines all over town and brought Nashville to a standstill. Then, eight inches of snow fell on Tuesday, making it impossible for Paul and Zeke to leave. By Wednesday morning Paul and Zeke had spent all their money, bringing their sexual privileges and drinking to an end. But Della allowed them stay on without charging them for meals or for sleeping on the floor in front of the fireplace. In fact, everyone slept in the parlor because the electricity didn't come back on for several days. The thaw didn't come for over a week and it was the following Tuesday when Paul and Zeke finally managed to clear the snow and ice from their truck and head out for Kentucky. The storm became known as the "Blizzard of 51" and was considered the worst in the recorded history of Tennessee.

As the word spread, Della's business increased dramatically, and by the end of 1953, hers was one of the most popular and well known brothels in the Southeast. It was a success from day one, just as she had predicted, but to her surprise, business at the bar took off like a rocket.

Unlike at Pauline's where a customer might down one for the road prior to heading home, the house on Russell Street quickly became one of the most popular watering holes in the city. In Nashville there were laws on the books that prohibited the sale of liquor by the drink, but of course alcohol flowed freely in most of the clubs around town, especially in Printer's Alley, the infamous row of after hours clubs that sprang up in the early forties, replacing the string of print shops that gave the alley its name. And just as they did regarding the ready availability of alcohol in the alley, law enforcement and politicians turned a blind eye to the illegal activities at Della's, both upstairs and down. Della hadn't planned on operating the bar as a separate enterprise, but rather as a convenience for her upstairs customers, and to perhaps pick up a few extra dollars. It soon became, however, one of the best known secrets in town. It was a place where Politicians and off-duty police officers felt more free to relax than they did in the public establishments downtown. At Della's, they worried less about being seen. And unlike the lounges of downtown, Della's place didn't collect a cover charge for merely coming through the door. Selling alcohol was illegal, but so was prostitution and Della felt no more at risk running one business than the other. Customers were allowed to *brownbag* in clubs all over town, which meant they could bring a bottle with them, check it at the bar and then buy cocktails made with their own liquor. This was a win-win proposition for the club owners who were in effect selling alcohol back to the customers who had provided it to begin with. Della maintained a well stocked bar, and since her business operated outside the law, not having a liquor license was of no concern. She had an arrangement with a local distributor who sold her case after case of liquor at wholesale prices plus five percent for delivery. An illegal cocktail could easily be had at any club in town for a dollar and fifty cents, so Della priced all her drinks for one-dollar. She also offered the added attraction of readily available girls, a feature with which the downtown clubs could not easily compete. By the summer of 1954, Della maintained a crew of eight girls who were kept busy seven days a week. She had three part-timers who filled in during the regulars' monthly *sabbaticals*, as well as a waiting list of five.

Della hit the jackpot one Saturday morning when twin, red-haired sisters showed up at her door looking for work. Dixie and Zelda Goldman were the progeny of a Jewish-Irish-American union of a successful Miami attorney and a former New Orleans stripper. The Goldman twins were graduate students at Vanderbilt University where both were pursuing doctorates in clinical psychology. They claimed their interest in prostitution to be purely academic, and an integral part of their studies, but they threw themselves enthusiastically into their work and would often tag-team clients, leaving them euphoric and exhausted. Dixie and Zelda were only available on weekends because of their busy school schedules and soon cultivated a Saturday and Sunday clientele so extensive they became available by appointment only. A date with the Goldman twins was expensive, but memorable, and over a two-year period they earned a healthy profit for Della and Beatrice, and they enough money for themselves to buy matching Mercedes Benz convertibles.

Beatrice answered a knock at the door one warm, spring Monday morning to find a very attractive and well dressed lady who appeared nervous, looking all around like she was afraid of being seen.

"Are you Della?" she asked.

"No, my name is Beatrice, would you like to come inside?" The lady hurriedly stepped inside and seemed relieved when Beatrice closed the door behind her. She introduced herself as Jessica.

"This is awkward for me," she said, "so, I'll just come to the point. I'm looking for work."

"Well, you've certainly come to the right place, have you

done this before, I mean, have you ever worked in a brothel?"

"No, I haven't and I'm not looking to live and work here like your other girls. I can't, you see, I'm . . . well I'm married and I'm only available in the daytime. I can't be gone from home at night and I can't work at a place like this for fear of being seen by someone who knows me."

"I see," said Beatrice "then what is it you have in mind?"

"Well, I thought maybe you could set me up by appointment to meet clients somewhere more private, like in hotel rooms. But I wouldn't want to go to places like those dumps on Dickerson Road. You know . . . maybe somewhere a little more dignified, like the Maxwell House or the Noel."

"That would make you a call girl," said Bea, "and although we haven't done anything like that before, I don't see a problem. If you don't mind my asking, why are you wanting to do this? Do you need money? Do you have a gambling problem or something? You're married, and by the looks of your clothes, I'd say you're doing very well. I'm just curious to know why you want to do this."

"Well, that's not an easy question to answer. I guess you

could say that men aren't the only ones who don't get what they need at home."

Jessica Pemberton was the wife of Nashville attorney, Frederick Pemberton, a ne'er-do-well junior partner in the firm of Pemberton, Pemberton and Mahoney; his father, his uncle and his uncle by marriage. The Pemberton brothers formed the partnership back in the early thirties and slowly built it into one of Nashville's premier law firms by winning a string of high-profile cases that brought in big dollars. Frederick's father, Jackson, and his uncle Timothy were both graduates of the YMCA School of Law that was formed in Nashville back in 1911 and provided an alternative to the more traditional institutions like Vanderbilt. Students at this *working man's* law school attended classes at night and paid tuition fees that were pennies compared to those of the more prestigious schools. Frederick graduated from The Vanderbilt School of Law because his father could afford the tuition that he'd been unable to scrape together for himself. But sadly, Jackson Pemberton passed his wealth on to his son and nothing else; certainly not his work ethic nor his integrity. Fredrick flaunted his Vanderbilt education like a badge of snobbery, and readily shoved it into anyone's face who had the patience to listen to him for more than thirty-seconds. Outwardly he was gracious, but he looked down on almost everyone, even his own father and uncle because of their blue-collar law degrees. But it was Jessica, his wife of twelve years, who suffered the brunt of his condescending arrogance.

Jessica suspected for years that Freddy was cheating on her, but she'd never caught him in the act, and she had no way to prove it. He was no longer attentive to her needs and seldom engaged her in sex, never mind conversation, whereas early in their marriage they often talked well into the night after making love. She finally reached the point that she no longer loved or cared for Freddy and made the decision to take responsibility for her own happiness. She wanted to leave him, but was unwilling to give up her home, and she knew that a court battle would prove futile and that she would be left penniless. Turning to prostitution was her only hope to earn the money she needed to free herself from the hopeless situation.

"Here's what we can do," Beatrice said to her. "I can spread the word around in some of the better hotels that you are available, say on a couple of hour's notice, if that's enough time for you. I'll tell them you're available for a quickie or for the whole day, but that you have to be out of there by what time, five o'clock?"

"I'm listening," said Jessica, "and so far it sounds good."

"Through my connections with some of the bellmen, we

can screen the clients to make sure you're not gettin' hooked up with some freak, and to also be sure you get your money. And oh yeah, be sure you always get the money up front. Speaking of money, we need to discuss the terms of our arrangement. Of course you'll have travel time and such, so what do you think about thirty dollars for a quickie and say, one-hundred for the entire afternoon. We get sixty percent of the money here, but of course we furnish the house and the girls' room and board, so how bout we take thirty percent for setting everything up and you keep seventy. Does that sound reasonable?"

The arrangement with Jessica turned out to be an overwhelming success and opened the door to a lucrative call girl operation, conceived and run by Beatrice. Jessica stayed busy with all the appointments she could handle, and as word spread through the Nashville business community, demand for high-dollar prostitutes grew by leaps and bounds. Bellmen at The Noel, The Maxwell House and the exclusive Hermitage Hotel soon got word to Beatrice that more girls were needed to accommodate the big spenders who relied on the bellmen to supply their entertainment. Jessica enticed a couple of her coffee-klatch friends with tales of easy money and the allure of illicit sex with strangers.

The number of ladies working for Della and Beatrice soon numbered close to thirty, including the eleven who worked at the house on Russell Street. There were only eight bedrooms, but the girls rotated in shifts of three weeks each as nature dictated. The business continued to grow steadily, and by the close of the nineteen-fifties, Della and Beatrice had accumulated a small fortune. Beatrice was managing appointments for more than fifteen call girls, some of them fetching upwards of one-hundred dollars an hour. The bar stayed packed every night of the week, and in 1959 alone, Della and Beatrice shared profits of over one-hundred thousand dollars each.

Ask not what your country can do for you! Proclaimed the gorgeous new hunk of a president, from the television screen. *Ask what you can do for your country!*

"Ask what I can do for you, sweet-cakes," Beatrice cooed at the television screen, "and I promise you'll not go away disappointed!"

Beatrice was seldom excited over any man. iIn fact, she'd had her fill of men and all the crap that comes with them. But JFK rekindled a fire inside her that she'd long since thought was permanently extinguished.

"Now there's a man worth having!" she said to Della,

knowing nothing of the young president's adulterous escapades.

It was no secret that Beatrice had had her fill of men, but there was that one time back in 1952, right after they'd opened the business, that an unbelievably handsome man came in, and after meticulously inspecting each girl, he noticed Beatrice. Unlike the others, Bea was fully dressed and obviously not part of the menu, but the young Adonis walked to where she was sitting, stood quietly for a moment staring at her and finally asked, "How much for you?"

Her face turned red as her hair. She sat silently for a moment, then rose from the sofa and took his hand.

"Come on honey," she said. "When we're done you can pay me whatever you think it was worth." She led him into her bedroom and closed the door, and that was the only time Beatrice ever entertained a client . . . at least that anyone knew of.

Pauline Tabor once boasted of entertaining countless state and local officials, several US Congressmen and one US President, though she never named names. Della Borden couldn't claim to have hosted a president, but after ten years in business, she had watched more than her share of local politicians climb the *stairway to heaven*, as well as three members of the US House of Representatives. Beatrice wracked her brain trying to figure a way to get a personal invitation to JFK, but found it impossible. She never got over her infatuation with the man, nor the heartbreak she suffered on November 22, 1963.

The Metro Nashville City Council approved the sale of alcohol for on-premises consumption in 1968, which meant that cocktails could be sold legally in bars and restaurants throughout the city. The bar at *Della's*, as the house on Russell Street became affectionately known, remained open but suffered a serious decline in sales when the new, high-end establishments sprang up across Nashville, triggered by the lure of huge profits from the sale of alcohol. Della and Beatrice, with the help of their bookkeeper and tax consultant, calculated that the space being occupied by the back-porch bar would be better utilized as additional bedrooms.

News coverage of the infamous Woodstock Festival filled the television screen in 1969 with images of hundreds of half naked hippies cavorting in the mud and leaving viewers wondering what was going on that wasn't being shown on camera. Even though Della and Beatrice were in no position to question the morals of others, they couldn't help but raise an eyebrow at the questionable behavior of the raucous youngsters. Kids were different now, more so than in the past, when such indiscretion was kept private.

"You see what's going on, don't you?" Bea asked Della, as the ten-o'clock news signed off. "What?" said Della, "I saw a lot of kids parading around half naked, if that's what you mean."

"Yeah, that's exactly what I mean, but do you realize the effect it's gonna have on us?"

"I don't get what you're sayin' Bea, what're you talkin' about?"

"The girls, Della, look how they're dressed and how they act. They have no shame, they're all runnin' around braless, everything floppin' around for the whole world to see and they're not the least bit shy about it!"

"Yeah, but what's that got to do with us?"

"It's all that *free love* stuff. Don't you see, these girls all claim to be liberated, that means they're all screwing around. Girls today don't think anything of it, they're not like we were at their age, they're not holding anything back. Most young guys won't have to come to places like this if they're gettin' all they want for free. You mark my words, we're gonna see fewer and fewer young guys coming here to spend their money because they just won't need us. We'll still get our share of the losers, of course, but you won't be seeing many of the cute ones anymore."

Della seldom thought of Bill McMasters, the *Alan* she'd met at Pauline's, and with whom she'd fallen in love. But in 1974, McMasters decided to run for mayor and suddenly his face was plastered on posters all over the city. It hurt Della's heart to see his face and to think of the nights she'd spent in his arms, but those were memories from the past and that's where they belonged. She attended a rally for McMasters in Shelby Park where she managed to work her way into the second row, within a few feet of where he was standing. After his speech, he mingled with the crowd, shaking hands and kissing babies, and when he took Della's hand, he gave it a special squeeze acknowledging the high regard he still held for her. She leaned forward onto her tiptoes, kissed him on the cheek and whispered in his ear that she missed him, and that she had every intention of voting for him as many times as she possibly could.

"I miss you too," he whispered, then exploded into laughter at her humorous side that he had never seen.

In less than a week, another rally was held for McMasters in front of East Nashville High School on Gallatin Avenue, where from the front steps he made a rousing speech vowing to declare war on crime in Nashville, if elected.

"You gonna shut down that whorehouse over on Russell Street?" cried a disheveled old lady in the crowd.

"I'll shut down that place and every one like it in Nashville if I'm elected mayor!" he declared, having no idea at the time the old woman was talking about Della's until an aide, who was one of Della's regulars, slipped him a note on which was written the address of the place. Back in his office at the courthouse, the judge looked in the record of deeds and found Della Borden listed as the owner of that particular property. He requested an investigation into the allegation made by the lady in the crowd, and after a few phone calls, two officers from the vice division of the Metro Police Department were dispatched to the house on Russell Street. When their investigation turned up no evidence of wrongdoing, they reported back to the head of the vice division, who reported to the Judge, who reported to the four local news channels that the house on Russell Street was the headquarters of a Christian association dedicated to helping wayward young women learn to live productive lives and become upstanding citizens.

Judge McMasters, along with the current mayor, went on live television and offered an apology to the residents of the faith-based home and advised the citizens of Nashville to be more cognizant of the potential harm to innocent people that can be so easily inflicted by idle gossip and hurtful rumors.

As it happened, on the night before the raid by the Metro Vice Squad, Della received an anonymous phone call advising her of the impending investigation and the approximate time the police would arrive. When the two officers knocked on the front door, they were greeted by the founder of the association, *Pastor* Della Borden and her assistant, *Sister* Beatrice Fuller. Beatrice offered coffee to the officers and politely invited them to join in the Bible study that was currently underway in the parlor. The officers declined the coffee, as well as the invitation, and after a quick stroll through the rooms on the first floor, they apologized to the roomful of prudishly dressed young women and left the house. On his way out, the ranking officer of the two, smiled and winked at Della as he closed the door behind him.

It was in the spring of 1980 that Della and Beatrice first heard about the outbreak in San Francisco of the disease that the news anchor referred to as *AIDS*.

This disease is thought to have originated in Africa as far back as the nineteen-twenties, the reporter said, *and is believed to have been introduced into to this country by*

members of the homosexual community. We are told by
the CDC that there is no known cure for AIDS and that
the disease has proven terminal in every case heretofore
diagnosed.

"That's gonna do us in," said Beatrice. "That's a whole different ball game than a case of the clap or syphilis. A shot of penicillin ain't gonna clear up that shit."

"You really think it'll hurt us?" asked Della.

"Maybe not tomorrow, maybe not even next year, but just you wait! When everybody gets good and scared of getting AIDS, we won't be able find a girl anywhere who'll be willing to run the risk of taking on anybody and everybody who walks through that door. According to what I've heard and read, you can't detect AIDS like you can the others, at least not in the early stages. I know I wouldn't risk it, would you?"

Little by little, the prostitution business dwindled to near extinction, at least in the better houses. Word was, that many high-dollar call girls were staying busy, but those were the thousand-dollar-a-night variety who carefully picked and chose a clientele not likely to travel in the same circles as those prone to exposure to the HIV virus. But still, there were no guarantees. All the girls who had once worked for Della and Beatrice had moved on after socking away enormous sums of money, or they had simply gotten too old, and there were no young girls stepping up to replace them. The loosening standards of morality triggered a decline in the demand for commercial affection, and the threat of more virulent STD's, as well as AIDS, the big daddy of them all, virtually put an end to widespread, casual sex. By the middle nineteen-eighties, the AIDS epidemic accomplished what law enforcement and legions of do-gooders had failed to do since the beginning of time; it brought the world's oldest profession to a virtual standstill. Once-glorious houses like Pauline's and Della's soon became relics, and the only hookers available to the average Joe were the hopelessly addicted crack-whores that no man in his right mind would dare touch.

Della put the house on the market and it quickly sold to an organization that, of all things, purchased the multi-bedroom home for use as a rehabilitative group home for women who were addicted to drugs, most of them by pimps who had used and abused them for financial gain. Della and Beatrice were both independently wealthy after more than thirty-five years in the business, and settled comfortably into lives of leisure.

"We had a good run, didn't we!" said Della, clinking

glasses of orange juice and champagne in a toast on the terrace of their beachfront home on the Alabama coast.

"Do you have any regrets?" Beatrice asked. Della stared at the waves breaking onto the white sand, then turned up the glass and downed the last swallow.

"I wish I'd met Alan, or *Bill* that is, under different circumstances. I really loved that man and I think he could've loved me. I wish we'd had kids together."

"You never told me much about him," said Bea. "And I'm curious. What makes you think it would have worked?"

"When he told me back in Bowling Green that he was getting married, I never saw him again until that day on the courthouse steps when I bought the place on Russell Street. He knew how to find me any time he wanted, but I guess he never wanted to. He was married, and evidently, remained faithful to his wife. And he knew when we opened the house on Russell Street, but in all those years he never once stepped foot into the place. He was a good man . . . the only one I ever knew that I wish I could have kept."

Della's mother died in 1947, then Maureen in '61. Nora passed on in 1967 and Francine died of liver cancer in 1980. They were all buried in the cemetery at Cash Point, on the outskirts of Ardmore, Tennessee. Della lost touch with her brothers and hadn't seen or heard from any of them since that night she saw Martin at Pauline's.

"Wanna take a ride?" she asked Beatrice. "I need to see my family, you wanna come with me?"

"Your family?" said Bea. "I thought they were all dead . . . at least the ones you know about."

"They are, but I need to go back there one more time."

"You mean you're going to Podunk?" asked Bea, then flashed her still gorgeous smile.

"Yeah, Podunk," said Della. "You really need to see it."

They left just before sunup and crossed intoTennessee a little after 1:00 p.m. Della stopped at a flower shop in Ardmore and bought four white roses to place onto the graves of her mother and three sisters.

"You know, I bet those are the first flowers any of them ever got in their whole lives. I don't reckon mama ever had much of anything nice, and I know for certain that my sisters didn't." She walked to the foot of her daddy's grave and stared at the headstone.

"I don't remember my daddy," she said. "But he was a good lookin' rascal. Mama used to keep his picture in an old cedar chest, and sometimes I'd get it out and look at it. I don't know what ever happened to that picture, *or* the cedar chest for that matter. I think maybe some of my brothers and their wives went through all that stuff after Francine died."

They left the cemetery and drove to the abandoned old schoolhouse at Cash Point, and it was from there Della retraced her childhood footsteps to the field where the tiny house once stood. They sat in Della's Mercedes with the air conditioning on low and watched the gigantic machine make its way across the field, covering several rows with each pass.

"That thing can do more in one hour than a dozen field-hands can in a week." Della said. "And right over there, just on the other side of those trees is a big sinkhole, and a few hundred feet this side of it is where I lived when I was a kid. The house was right there in the middle of that field."

"Pardon me for sayin' so honey," said Bea. "But this looks like a shitty place to live, especially for a kid."

"It was," said Della. "It was the shittiest place on earth."

About the Author

Doyle Petty is a native Tennessean and lives in Nashville with Judy, his wife, Bobby, a Parson Russell Terrier and Jimmy, a rescued cat. He attended Franklin High School and graduated from Cohn High School in Nashville and Austin Peay State University in Clarksville, Tennessee where he majored in Accounting.